THE HOUSE ON THE BEACH:

A REALISTIC TALE

By

GEORGE MEREDITH

Double9
BOOKS

The House on The Beach:
A Realistic Tale

by George Meredith

Copyright © 2023

ISBN: 978-93-57484-68-8

Published by

DOUBLE 9 BOOKS

2/13-B, Ansari Road, Daryaganj
New Delhi – 110002
info@double9books.com
www.double9books.com
Tel. 011-40042856

ABOUT THE AUTHOR

George Meredith OM (February 12, 1828-May 18, 1909) was born in Portsmouth, United Kingdom. He was an English poet, writer, and author, whose books are noted for their intelligence, extraordinary dialogues, and aphoristic way of writing. Meredith's books are also recognised for psychological studies of character and a highly subjective perspective on life that is a long way ahead of its time, considering women are equals to men in all streams. His most popular works are The Ordeal of Richard Feverel (1859) and The Egoist (1879). He was nominated for the Nobel Prize in Literature seven times.

CONTENTS

CHAPTER I

The experience of great officials who have laid down their dignities before death, or have had the philosophic mind to review themselves while still wielding the deputy sceptre, teaches them that in the exercise of authority over men an eccentric behaviour in trifles has most exposed them to hostile criticism and gone farthest to jeopardize their popularity. It is their Achilles' heel; the place where their mother Nature holds them as she dips them in our waters. The eccentricity of common persons is the entertainment of the multitude, and the maternal hand is perceived for a cherishing and endearing sign upon them; but rarely can this be found suitable for the august in station; only, indeed, when their sceptre is no more fearful than a grandmother's birch; and these must learn from it sooner or later that they are uncomfortably mortal.

When herrings are at auction on a beach, for example, the man of chief distinction in the town should not step in among a poor fraternity to take advantage of an occasion of cheapness, though it be done, as he may protest, to relieve the fishermen of a burden; nor should such a dignitary as the bailiff of a Cinque Port carry home the spoil of victorious bargaining on his arm in a basket. It is not that his conduct is in itself objectionable, so much as that it causes him to be popularly weighed; and during life, until the best of all advocates can plead before our fellow Englishmen that we are out of their way, it is prudent to avoid the process.

Mr. Tinman, however, this high-stepping person in question, happened to have come of a marketing mother. She had started him from a small shop to a big one. He, by the practice of her virtues, had been enabled to start himself as a gentleman. He was a man of this ambition, and prouder behind it. But having started himself precipitately, he took rank among independent incomes, as they are called, only to take fright at the perils of starvation besetting one who has been tempted to abandon the source of fifty per cent. So, if noble imagery were allowable in our time in prose, might alarms and partial regrets be assumed to animate the splendid pumpkin cut loose from the suckers. Deprived of that prodigious nourishment of the shop in the fashionable seaport of Helmstone, he retired upon his native town, the Cinque Port of Crikswich, where he rented the cheapest residence he could discover for his habitation, the House on the Beach, and lived imposingly, though not in total disaccord with his old mother's principles. His income, as he observed to his widowed sister and solitary companion almost daily in their privacy, was respectable. The descent from an altitude of fifty to five per cent. cannot but be felt. Nevertheless it was a comforting midnight bolster reflection for a man, turning over to the other side between a dream and a wink, that he was making no bad debts, and one must pay to be addressed as esquire. Once an esquire, you are off the ground in England and on the ladder. An esquire can offer his hand in marriage to a lady in her own right; plain esquires have married duchesses; they marry baronets' daughters every day of the week.

Thoughts of this kind were as the rise and fall of waves in the bosom of the new esquire. How often in his Helmstone shop had he not heard titled ladies disdaining to talk a whit more prettily than ordinary women; and he had been a match for the subtlety of their pride—he understood it. He knew well that at the hint of a proposal from him they would have spoken out in a manner very different to that of ordinary women. The lightning, only to be warded by an esquire, was in them. He quitted business at the age of forty, that he might pretend to espousals with a born lady; or at least it was one of the ideas in his mind.

And here, I think, is the moment for the epitaph of anticipation over him, and the exclamation, alas! I would not be premature, but it is necessary to create some interest in him, and no one but a foreigner could feel it at present for the Englishman who is bursting merely to do like the rest of his countrymen, and rise above them to shake them class by class as the dust from his heels. Alas! then an—undertaker's pathos is better than none at all—he was not a single-minded aspirant to our social honours. The old marketing mother, to whom he owed his fortunes, was in his blood to confound his ambition; and so contradictory was the man's nature, that in revenge for disappointments, there were times when he turned against the saving spirit of parsimony. Readers deep in Greek dramatic writings will see the fatal Sisters behind the chair of a man who gives frequent and bigger dinners, that he may become important in his neighbourhood, while decreasing the price he pays for his wine, that he may miserably indemnify himself for the outlay. A sip of his wine fetched the breath, as when men are in the presence of the tremendous elements of nature. It sounded the constitution more darkly-awful, and with a profounder testimony to stubborn health, than the physician's instruments. Most of the guests at Mr. Tinman's table were so constructed that they admired him for its powerful quality the more at his announcement of the price of it; the combined strength and cheapness probably flattering them, as by another mystic instance of the national energy. It must have been so, since his townsmen rejoiced to hail him as head of their town. Here and there a solitary esquire, fished out of the bathing season to dine at the house on the beach, was guilty of raising one of those clamours concerning subsequent headaches, which spread an evil reputation as a pall. A resident esquire or two, in whom a reminiscence of Tinman's table may be likened to the hook which some old trout has borne away from the angler as the most vivid of warnings to him to beware for the future, caught up the black report and propagated it.

The Lieutenant of the Coastguard, hearing the latest conscious victim, or hearing of him, would nod his head and say he had never dined at Tinman's table without a headache ensuing and a visit to the chemist's shop; which, he was assured, was good for trade, and he acquiesced, as it was right to do in a man devoted to his country. He dined with Tinman again. We try our best to be social. For eight months in our year he had little choice but to dine with Tinman or be a hermit attached to a telescope.

"Where are you going, Lieutenant?" His frank reply to the question was, "I am going to be killed;" and it grew notorious that this meant Tinman's table. We get on together as well as we can. Perhaps if we were an acutely calculating people we should find it preferable both for trade and our physical prosperity to turn and kill Tinman, in contempt of consequences. But we are not, and so he does the business gradually for us. A generous people we must be, for Tinman was not detested. The recollection of "next morning" caused him to be dimly feared.

Tinman, meanwhile, was awake only to the Circumstance that he made no progress as an esquire, except on the envelopes of letters, and in his own esteem. That broad region he began to occupy to the exclusion of other inhabitants; and the result of such a state of princely isolation was a plunge of his whole being into deep thoughts. From the hour of his investiture as the town's chief man, thoughts which were long shots took possession of him. He had his wits about him; he was alive to ridicule; he knew he was not popular below, or on easy terms with people above him, and he meditated a surpassing stroke as one of the Band of Esq., that had nothing original about it to perplex and annoy the native mind, yet was dazzling. Few members of the privileged Band dare even imagine the thing.

It will hardly be believed, but it is historical fact, that in the act of carrying fresh herrings home on his arm, he entertained the idea of a visit to the First Person and Head of the realm, and was indulging in pleasing visions of the charms of a personal acquaintance. Nay, he had already consulted with brother jurats. For you must know that one of the princesses had recently suffered betrothal in the newspapers, and supposing her to deign to ratify the engagement, what so reasonable on the part of a Cinque Port chieftain as to congratulate his liege mistress, her illustrious mother? These are thoughts and these are deeds >which give emotional warmth and colour to the ejecter members of a population wretchedly befogged. They are our sunlight, and our brighter theme of conversation. They are necessary to the climate and the Saxon mind; and it would be foolish to put them away, as it is foolish not to do our utmost to be intimate with terrestrial splendours while we have them—as it may be said of wardens, mayors, and bailiffs-at command. Tinman was quite of this opinion. They are there to relieve our dulness. We have them in the place of heavenly; and he would have argued that we have a right to bother them too. He had a notion, up in the clouds, of a Sailors' Convalescent Hospital at Crikswich to seduce a prince with, hand him the trowel, make him "lay the stone," and then poor prince! refresh him at table. But that was a matter for by and by.

His purchase of herrings completed, Mr. Tinman walked across the mound of shingle to the house on the beach. He was rather a fresh-faced man, of the Saxon colouring, and at a distance looking good-humoured. That he should have been able to make such an appearance while doing daily battle with his wine, was a proof of great physical vigour. His pace was leisurely, as it must needs be over pebbles, where half a step is subtracted from each whole one in passing; and, besides, he was aware of a general breath at his departure that betokened a censorious assembly. Why should he not market for himself? He threw dignity into his retreating figure in response to the internal interrogation. The moment >was one when conscious rectitude =pliers man should have a tail for its just display. Philosophers have drawn attention to the power of the human face to express pure virtue, but no sooner has it passed on than the spirit erect within would seem helpless. The breadth of our shoulders is apparently presented for our critics to write on. Poor duty is done by the simple sense of moral worth, to supplant that absence of feature in the plain flat back. We are below the animals in this. How charged with language behind him is a dog! Everybody has noticed it. Let a dog turn away from a hostile circle, and his crisp and wary tail not merely defends him, it menaces; it is a weapon. Man has no choice but to surge and boil, or stiffen preposterously. Knowing the popular sentiment about his marketing—for men can see behind their backs, though they may have nothing to speak with—Tinman resembled those persons of principle who decline to pay for a "Bless your honour!" from a voluble beggar-woman, and obtain the reverse of it after they have gone by. He was sufficiently sensitive to feel that his back was chalked as on a slate. The only remark following him was, "There he goes!"

He went to the seaward gate of the house on the beach, made practicable in a low flint wall, where he was met by his sister Martha, to whom he handed the basket. Apparently he named the cost of his purchase per dozen. She touched the fish and pressed the bellies of the topmost, it might be to question them tenderly concerning their roes. Then the couple passed out of sight. Herrings were soon after this despatching their odours through the chimneys of all Crikswich, and there was that much of concord and festive union among the inhabitants.

The house on the beach had been posted where it stood, one supposes, for the sake of the sea-view, from which it turned right about to face the town across a patch of grass and salt scurf, looking like a square and scornful corporal engaged in the perpetual review of an awkward squad of recruits. Sea delighted it not, nor land either. Marine Parade fronting it to the left, shaded sickly eyes, under a worn green verandah, from a sun that rarely appeared, as the traducers of spinsters pretend those virgins are ever keenly on their guard against him that cometh not. Belle Vue Terrace stared out of lank glass panes without reserve, unashamed of its yellow complexion. A gaping public-house, calling itself newly Hotel, fell backward a step. Villas with the titles of royalty and bloody battles claimed five feet of garden, and swelled in bowwindows beside other villas which drew up firmly, commending to the attention a decent straightness and unintrusive decorum in preference. On an elevated meadow to the right was the Crouch. The Hall of Elba nestled among weather-beaten dwarf woods further toward the cliff. Shavenness, featurelessness, emptiness, clamminess scurfiness, formed the outward expression of a town to which people were reasonably glad to come from London in summer-time, for there was nothing in Crikswich to distract the naked pursuit of health. The sea tossed its renovating brine to the determinedly sniffing animal, who went to his meals with an appetite that rendered him cordially eulogistic of the place, in spite of certain frank whiffs of sewerage coming off an open deposit on the common to mingle with the brine. Tradition told of a French lady and gentleman entering the town to take lodgings for a month, and that on the morrow they took a boat from the shore, saying in their faint English to a sailor veteran of the coastguard, whom they had consulted about the weather, "It is better zis zan zat," as they shrugged between rough sea and corpselike land. And they were not seen again. Their meaning none knew. Having paid their bill at the lodging-house, their conduct was ascribed to systematic madness. English people came to Crikswich for the pure salt sea air, and they did not expect it to be cooked and dressed and decorated for them. If these things are done to nature, it is nature no longer that you have, but something Frenchified. Those French are for trimming Neptune's beard! Only wait, and you are sure to find variety in nature, more than you may like. You will find it in Neptune. What say you to a breach of the sea-wall, and an inundation of the aromatic grass- flat extending from the house on the beach to the tottering terraces, villas, cottages: and public-house transformed by its ensign to Hotel, along the frontage of the town? Such an event had occurred of old, and had given the house on the beach the serious shaking great Neptune in his wrath alone can give. But many years had intervened. Groynes had been run down to intercept him and divert him. He generally did his winter mischief on a mill and salt marshes lower westward. Mr. Tinman had always been extremely zealous in promoting the expenditure of what moneys the town had to spare upon the protection of the shore, as it were for the propitiation or defiance of the sea-god. There was a kindly joke against him an that subject among brother jurats. He retorted with the joke, that the first thing for Englishmen to look to were England's defences.

But it will not do to be dwelling too fondly on our eras of peace, for which we make such splendid sacrifices. Peace, saving for the advent of a German band, which troubled the repose of the town at intervals, had imparted to the inhabitants of Crikswich, within and without, the likeness to its most perfect image, together, it must be confessed, with a degree of nervousness that invested common events with some of the terrors of the Last Trump, when one night, just upon the passing of the vernal equinox, something happened.

CHAPTER II

A carriage Stopped short in the ray of candlelight that was fitfully and feebly capering on the windy blackness outside the open workshop of Crickledon, the carpenter, fronting the sea-beach. Mr. Tinnnan's house was inquired for. Crickledon left off planing; at half-sprawl over the board, he bawled out, "Turn to the right; right ahead; can't mistake it." He nodded to one of the cronies intent on watching his labours: "Not unless they mean to be bait for whiting-pout. Who's that for Tinman, I wonder?" The speculations of Crickledon's friends were lost in the scream of the plane.

One cast an eye through the door and observed that the carriage was there still. "Gentleman's got out and walked," said Crickledon. He was informed that somebody was visible inside. "Gentleman's wife, mayhap," he said. His friends indulged in their privilege of thinking what they liked, and there was the usual silence of tongues in the shop. He furnished them sound and motion for their amusement, and now and then a scrap of conversation; and the sedater spirits dwelling in his immediate neighbourhood were accustomed to step in and see him work up to supper- time, instead of resorting to the more turbid and costly excitement of the public-house.

Crickledon looked up from the measurement of a thumb-line. In the doorway stood a bearded gentleman, who announced himself with the startling exclamation, "Here's a pretty pickle!" and bustled to make way for a man well known to them as Ned Crummins, the upholsterer's man, on whose back hung an article of furniture, the condition of which, with a condensed brevity of humour worthy of literary admiration, he displayed by mutely turning himself about as he entered.

"Smashed!" was the general outcry.

"I ran slap into him," said the gentleman. "Who the deuce!—no bones broken, that's one thing. The fellow—there, look at him: he's like a glass tortoise."

"It's a chiwal glass," Crickledon remarked, and laid finger on the star in the centre.

"Gentleman ran slap into me," said Crummins, depositing the frame on the floor of the shop.

"Never had such a shock in my life," continued the gentleman. "Upon my soul, I took him for a door: I did indeed. A kind of light flashed from one of your houses here, and in the pitch dark I thought I was at the door of old Mart Tinman's house, and dash me if I did n't go in—crash! But what the deuce do you do, carrying that great big looking-glass at night, man? And, look here tell me; how was it you happened to be going glass foremost when you'd got the glass on your back?"

"Well, 't ain't my fault, I knows that," rejoined Crummins. "I came along as careful as a man could. I was just going to bawl out to Master Tinman, 'I knows the way, never fear me'; for I thinks I hears him call from his house, 'Do ye see the way?' and into me this gentleman runs all his might, and smash goes the glass. I was just ten steps from Master Tinman's gate, and that careful, I reckoned every foot I put down, that I was; I knows I did, though."

"Why, it was me calling, 'I'm sure I can't see the way.'"

"You heard me, you donkey!" retorted the bearded gentleman. "What was the good of your turning that glass against me in the very nick when I dashed on you?"

"Well, 't ain't my fault, I swear," said Crummins. "The wind catches voices so on a pitch dark night, you never can tell whether they be on one shoulder or the other. And if I'm to go and lose my place through no fault of mine——"

"Have n't I told you, sir, I'm going to pay the damage? Here," said the gentleman, fumbling at his waistcoat, "here, take this card. Read it."

For the first time during the scene in the carpenter's shop, a certain pomposity swelled the gentleman's tone. His delivery of the card appeared to act on him like the flourish of a trumpet before great men.

"Van Diemen Smith," he proclaimed himself for the assistance of Ned Crummins in his task; the latter's look of sad concern on receiving the card seeming to declare an unscholarly conscience.

An anxious feminine voice was heard close beside Mr. Van Diemen Smith.

"Oh, papa, has there been an accident? Are you hurt?"

"Not a bit, Netty; not a bit. Walked into a big looking-glass in the dark, that's all. A matter of eight or ten pound, and that won't stump us. But these are what I call queer doings in Old England, when you can't take a step in the dark, on the seashore without plunging bang into a glass. And it looks like bad luck to my visit to old Mart Tinman."

"Can you," he addressed the company, "tell me of a clean, wholesome lodging-house? I was thinking of flinging myself, body and baggage, on your mayor, or whatever he is—my old schoolmate; but I don't so much like this beginning. A couple of bed-rooms and sitting-room; clean sheets, well aired; good food, well cooked; payment per week in advance."

The pebble dropped into deep water speaks of its depth by the tardy arrival of bubbles on the surface, and, in like manner, the very simple question put by Mr. Van Diemen Smith pursued its course of penetration in the assembled mind in the carpenter's shop for a considerable period, with no sign to show that it had reached the bottom.

"Surely, papa, we can go to an inn? There must be some hotel," said his daughter.

"There's good accommodation at the Cliff Hotel hard by," said Crickledon.

"But," said one of his friends, "if you don't want to go so far, sir, there's Master Crickledon's own house next door, and his wife lets lodgings, and there's not a better cook along this coast."

"Then why did n't the man mention it? Is he afraid of having me?" asked
Mr. Smith, a little thunderingly. "I may n't be known much yet in England; but I'll tell you, you inquire the route to Mr. Van Diemen Smith
over there in Australia."

"Yes, papa," interrupted his daughter, "only you must consider that it may not be convenient to take us in at this hour—so late."

"It's not that, miss, begging your pardon," said Crickledon. "I make a point of never recommending my own house. That's where it is. Otherwise you're welcome to try us."

"I was thinking of falling bounce on my old schoolmate, and putting Old
English hospitality to the proof," Mr. Smith meditated. "But it's late. Yes, and that confounded glass! No, we'll bide with you, Mr. Carpenter.
I'll send my card across to Mart Tinman to-morrow, and set him agog at
his breakfast."

Mr. Van Diemen Smith waved his hand for Crickledon to lead the way.

Hereupon Ned Crummins looked up from the card he had been turning over and over, more and more like one arriving at a condemnatory judgment of a fish.

"I can't go and give my master a card instead of his glass," he remarked.

"Yes, that reminds me; and I should like to know what you meant by bringing that glass away from Mr. Tinman's house at night," said Mr. Smith. "If I'm to pay for it, I've a right to know. What's the meaning of moving it at night? Eh, let's hear. Night's not the time for moving big glasses like that. I'm not so sure I haven't got a case."

"If you'll step round to my master along o' me, sir," said Crummins, "perhaps he'll explain."

Crummins was requested to state who his master was, and he replied, "Phippun and Company;" but Mr. Smith positively refused to go with him.

"But here," said he, "is a crown for you, for you're a civil fellow. You'll know where to find me in the morning; and mind, I shall expect Phippun and Company to give me a very good account of their reason for moving a big looking-glass on a night like this. There, be off."

The crown-piece in his hand effected a genial change in Crummins' disposition to communicate. Crickledon spoke to him about the glass; two or three of the others present jogged him. "What did Mr. Tinman want by having the glass moved so late in the day, Ned? Your master wasn't nervous about his property, was he?"

"Not he," said Crummins, and began to suck down his upper lip and agitate his eyelids and stand uneasily, glimmering signs of the setting in of the tide of narration.

He caught the eye of Mr. Smith, then looked abashed at Miss.

Crickledon saw his dilemma. "Say what's uppermost, Ned; never mind how you says it. English is English. Mr. Tinman sent for you to take the glass away, now, did n't he?"

"He did," said Crummins.

"And you went to him."

"Ay, that I did."

"And he fastened the chiwal glass upon your back"

"He did that."

"That's all plain sailing. Had he bought the glass?"

"No, he had n't bought it. He'd hired it."

As when upon an enforced visit to the dentist, people have had one tooth out, the remaining offenders are more willingly submitted to the operation, insomuch that a poetical licence might hazard the statement that they shed them like leaves of the tree, so Crummins, who had shrunk from speech, now volunteered whole sentences in succession, and how important they were deemed by his fellow-townsman, Mr. Smith, and especially Miss Annette Smith, could perceive in their ejaculations, before they themselves were drawn into the strong current of interest.

And this was the matter: Tinman had hired the glass for three days. Latish, on the very first day of the hiring, close upon dark, he had despatched imperative orders to Phippun and Company to take the glass out of his house on the spot. And why? Because, as he maintained, there was a fault in the glass causing an incongruous and absurd reflection; and he was at that moment awaiting the arrival of another chiwal-glass.

"Cut along, Ned," said Crickledon.

"What the deuce does he want with a chiwal-glass at all?" cried Mr. Smith, endangering the flow of the story by suggesting to the narrator that he must "hark back," which to him was equivalent to the jumping of a chasm hindward. Happily his brain had seized a picture:

"Mr. Tinman, he's a-standin' in his best Court suit."

Mr. Tinmau's old schoolmate gave a jump; and no wonder.

"Standing?" he cried; and as the act of standing was really not extraordinary, he fixed upon the suit: "Court?"

"So Mrs. Cavely told me, it was what he was standin' in, and as I found 'm I left 'm," said Crummins.

"He's standing in it now?" said Mr. Van Diemen Smith, with a great gape.

Crummins doggedly repeated the statement. Many would have ornamented it in the repetition, but he was for bare flat truth.

"He must be precious proud of having a Court suit," said Mr. Smith, and gazed at his daughter so glassily that she smiled, though she was impatient to proceed to Mrs. Crickledon's lodgings.

"Oh! there's where it is?" interjected the carpenter, with a funny frown at a low word from Ned Crummins. "Practicing, is he? Mr. Tinman's practicing before the glass preparatory to his going to the palace in London."

"He gave me a shillin'," said Crummins.

Crickledon comprehended him immediately. "We sha'n't speak about it,
Ned."

What did you see? was thus cautiously suggested.

The shilling was on Crummins' tongue to check his betrayal of the secret scene. But remembering that he had only witnessed it by accident, and that Mr. Tinman had not completely taken him into his confidence, he thrust his hand down his pocket to finger the crown-piece lying in fellowship with the coin it multiplied five times, and was inspired to think himself at liberty to say: "All I saw was when the door opened. Not the house-door. It was the parlour-door. I saw him walk up to the glass, and walk back from the glass. And when he'd got up to the glass he bowed, he did, and he went back'ards just so."

Doubtless the presence of a lady was the active agent that prevented Crummins from doubling his body entirely, and giving more than a rapid indication of the posture of Mr. Tinman in his retreat before the glass. But it was a glimpse of broad burlesque, and though it was received with becoming sobriety by the men in the carpenter's shop, Annette plucked at her father's arm.

She could not get him to depart. That picture of his old schoolmate Martin Tinman practicing before a chiwal glass to present himself at the palace in his Court suit, seemed to stupefy his Australian intelligence.

"What right has he got to go to Court?" Mr. Van Diemen Smith inquired, like the foreigner he had become through exile.

"Mr. Tinman's bailiff of the town," said Crickledon.

"And what was his objection to that glass I smashed?"

"He's rather an irritable gentleman," Crickledon murmured, and turned to
Crummins.

Crummins growled: "He said it was misty, and gave him a twist."

"What a big fool he must be! eh?" Mr. Smith glanced at Crickledon and the other faces for the verdict of Tinman's townsmen upon his character.

They had grounds for thinking differently of Tinman.

"He's no fool," said Crickledon.

Another shook his head. "Sharp at a bargain."

"That he be," said the chorus.

Mr. Smith was informed that Mr. Tinman would probably end by buying up half the town.

"Then," said Mr. Smith, "he can afford to pay half the money for that glass, and pay he shall."

A serious view of the recent catastrophe was presented by his declaration.

In the midst of a colloquy regarding the cost of the glass, during which it began to be seen by Mr. Tinman's townsmen that there was laughing- stuff for a year or so in the scene witnessed by Crummins, if they postponed a bit their right to the laugh and took it in doses, Annette induced her father to signal to Crickledon his readiness to go and see the lodgings. No sooner had he done it than he said, "What on earth made us wait all this time here? I'm hungry, my dear; I want supper."

"That is because you have had a disappointment. I know you, papa," said
Annette.

"Yes, it's rather a damper about old Mart Tinman," her father assented. "Or else I have n't recovered the shock of smashing that glass, and visit it on him. But, upon my honour, he's my only friend in England, I have n't a single relative that I know of, and to come and find your only friend making a donkey of himself, is enough to make a man think of eating and drinking."

Annette murmured reproachfully: "We can hardly say he is our only friend in England, papa, can we?"

"Do you mean that young fellow? You'll take my appetite away if you talk of him. He's a stranger. I don't believe he's worth a penny. He owns he's what he calls a journalist."

These latter remarks were hurriedly exchanged at the threshold of Crickledon's house.

"It don't look promising," said Mr. Smith.

"I didn't recommend it," said Crickledon.

"Why the deuce do you let your lodgings, then?"

"People who have come once come again."

"Oh! I am in England," Annette sighed joyfully, feeling at home in some trait she had detected in Crickledon.

CHAPTER III

The story of the shattered chiwal-glass and the visit of Tinman's old schoolmate fresh from Australia, was at many a breakfast-table before. Tinman heard a word of it, and when he did he had no time to spare for such incidents, for he was reading to his widowed sister Martha, in an impressive tone, at a tolerably high pitch of the voice, and with a suppressed excitement that shook away all things external from his mind as violently as it agitated his body. Not the waves without but the engine within it is which gives the shock and tremor to the crazy steamer, forcing it to cut through the waves and scatter them to spray; and so did Martin Tinman make light of the external attack of the card of VAN DIEMEN SMITH, and its pencilled line: "An old chum of yours, eh, matey? "Even the communication of Phippun & Co. concerning the chiwal- glass, failed to divert him from his particular task. It was indeed a public duty; and the chiwal-glass, though pertaining to it, was a private business. He that has broken the glass, let that man pay for it, he pronounced — no doubt in simpler fashion, being at his ease in his home, but with the serenity of one uplifted. As to the name VAN DIEMEN SMITH, he knew it not, and so he said to himself while accurately recollecting the identity of the old chum who alone of men would have thought of writing eh, matey?

Mr. Van Diemen Smith did not present the card in person. "At Crickledon's," he wrote, apparently expecting the bailiff of the town to rush over to him before knowing who he was.

Tinman was far too busy. Anybody can read plain penmanship or print, but ask anybody not a Cabinet Minister or a Lord-in-Waiting to read out loud and clear in a Palace, before a Throne. Oh! the nature of reading is distorted in a trice, and as Tinman said to his worthy sister: "I can do it, but I must lose no time in preparing myself." Again, at a reperusal, he informed her: "I must habituate myself." For this purpose he had put on the suit overnight.

The articulation of faultless English was his object. His sister Martha sat vice-regally to receive his loyal congratulations on the illustrious marriage, and she was pensive, less nervous than her brother from not having to speak continuously, yet somewhat perturbed. She also had her task, and it was to avoid thinking herself the Person addressed by her suppliant brother, while at the same time she took possession of the scholarly training and perfect knowledge of diction and rules of pronunciation which would infallibly be brought to bear on him in the terrible hour of the delivery of the Address. It was no small task moreover to be compelled to listen right through to the end of the Address, before the very gentlest word of criticism was allowed. She did not exactly complain of the renewal of the rehearsal: a fatigue can be endured when it is a joy. What vexed her was her failing memory for the points of objection, as in her imagined High Seat she conceived them; for, in painful truth, the instant her brother had finished she entirely lost her acuteness of ear, and with that her recollection: so there was nothing to do but to say: "Excellent! Quite unobjectionable, dear Martin, quite:" so she said, and emphatically; but the addition of the word "only" was printed on her contracted brow, and every faculty of Tinman's mind and nature being at strain just then, he asked her testily: "What now? what's the fault now?" She assured him with languor that there was not a fault. "It's not your way of talking," said he, and what he said was true. His discernment was extraordinary; generally he noticed nothing.

Not only were his perceptions quickened by the preparations for the day of great splendour: day of a great furnace to be passed through likewise! —he, was learning English at an astonishing rate into the bargain. A pronouncing Dictionary lay open on his table. To this he flew at a hint of a contrary method, and disputes, verifications and triumphs on one side and the other ensued between brother and sister. In his heart the agitated man believed his sister to be a misleading guide. He dared not say it, he thought it, and previous to his African travel through the Dictionary he had thought his sister infallible on these points. He dared not say it, because he knew no one else before whom he could practice, and as it was confidence that he chiefly wanted—above all things, confidence and confidence comes of practice, he preferred the going on with his practice to an absolute certainty as to correctness.

At midday came another card from Mr. Van Diemen Smith bearing the superscription: alias Phil R.

"Can it be possible," Tinman asked his sister, "that Philip Ribstone has had the audacity to return to this country? I think," he added, "I am right in treating whoever sends me this card as a counterfeit."

Martha's advice was, that he should take no notice of the card.

"I am seriously engaged," said Tinman. With a "Now then, dear," he resumed his labours.

Messages had passed between Tinman and Phippun; and in the afternoon Phippun appeared to broach the question of payment for the chiwal-glass. He had seen Mr. Van Diemen Smith, had found him very strange, rather impracticable. He was obliged to tell Tinman that he must hold him responsible for the glass; nor could he send a second until payment was made for the first. It really seemed as if Tinman would be compelled, by the force of circumstances, to go and shake his old friend by the hand. Otherwise one could clearly see the man might be off: he might be off at any minute, leaving a legal contention behind him. On the other hand, supposing he had come to Crikswich for assistance in money? Friendship is a good thing, and so is hospitality, which is an essentially English thing, and consequently one that it behoves an Englishman to think it his duty to perform, but we do not extend it to paupers. But should a pauper get so close to us as to lay hold of us, vowing he was once our friend, how shake him loose? Tinman foresaw that it might be a matter of five pounds thrown to the dogs, perhaps ten, counting the glass. He put on his hat, full of melancholy presentiments; and it was exactly half-past five o'clock of the spring afternoon when he knocked at Crickledon's door.

Had he looked into Crickledon's shop as he went by, he would have perceived Van Diemen Smith astride a piece of timber, smoking a pipe. Van Diemen saw Tinman. His eyes cocked and watered. It is a disgraceful fact to record of him without periphrasis. In truth, the bearded fellow was almost a woman at heart, and had come from the Antipodes throbbing to slap Martin Tinman on the back, squeeze his hand, run over England with him, treat him, and talk of old times in the presence of a trotting regiment of champagne. That affair of the chiwal-glass had temporarily damped his enthusiasm. The absence of a reply to his double transmission of cards had wounded him; and something in the look of Tinman disgusted his rough taste. But the well-known features recalled the days of youth. Tinman was his one living link to the country he admired as the conqueror of the world, and imaginatively delighted in as the seat of pleasures, and he could not discard the feeling of some love for Tinman without losing his grasp of the reason why, he had longed so fervently and travelled so breathlessly to return hither. In the days of their youth, Van Diemen had been Tinman's cordial spirit, at whom he sipped for cheerful visions of life, and a good honest glow of emotion now and then. Whether it was odd or not that the sipper should be oblivious, and the cordial spirit heartily reminiscent of those times, we will not stay to inquire.

Their meeting took place in Crickledon's shop. Tinman was led in by Mrs. Crickledon. His voice made a sound of metal in his throat, and his air was that of a man buttoned up to the palate, as he read from the card, glancing over his eyelids, "Mr. Van Diemen Smith, I believe."

"Phil Ribstone, if you like," said the other, without rising.

"Oh, ah, indeed!" Tinman temperately coughed.

"Yes, dear me. So it is. It strikes you as odd?"

"The change of name," said Tinman.

"Not nature, though!"

"Ah! Have you been long in England?"

"Time to run to Helmstone, and on here. You've been lucky in business,
I hear."

"Thank you; as things go. Do you think of remaining in England?"

"I've got to settle about a glass I broke last night."

"Ah! I have heard of it. Yes, I fear there will have to be a settlement."

"I shall pay half of the damage. You'll have to stump up your part."

Van Diemen smiled roguishly.

"We must discuss that," said Tinman, smiling too, as a patient in bed may smile at a doctor's joke; for he was, as Crickledon had said of him, no fool on practical points, and Van Diemen's mention of the half-payment reassured him as to his old friend's position in the world, and softly thawed him. "Will you dine with me to-day?"

"I don't mind if I do. I've a girl. You remember little Netty? She's walking out on the beach with a young fellow named Fellingham, whose acquaintance we made on the voyage, and has n't left us long to ourselves. Will you have her as well? And I suppose you must ask him. He's a newspaper man; been round the world; seen a lot."

Tinman hesitated. An electrical idea of putting sherry at fifteen shillings per dozen on his table instead of the ceremonial wine at twenty-five shillings, assisted him to say hospitably, "Oh! ah! yes; any friend of yours."

"And now perhaps you'll shake my fist," said Van Diemen.

"With pleasure," said Tinman. "It was your change of name, you know, Philip."

Look here, Martin. Van Diemen Smith was a convict, and my benefactor. Why the deuce he was so fond of that name, I can't tell you; but his dying wish was for me to take it and carry it on. He left me his fortune, for Van Diemen Smith to enjoy life, as he never did, poor fellow, when he was alive. The money was got honestly, by hard labour at a store. He did evil once, and repented after. But, by Heaven!" — Van Diemen jumped up and thundered out of a broad chest—"the man was one of the finest hearts that ever beat. He was! and I'm proud of him. When he died, I turned my thoughts home to Old England and you, Martin."

"Oh!" said Tinman; and reminded by Van Diemen's way of speaking, that cordiality was expected of him, he shook his limbs to some briskness, and continued, "Well, yes, we must all die in our native land if we can. I hope you're comfortable in your lodgings?"

"I'll give you one of Mrs. Crickledon's dinners to try. You're as good as mayor of this town, I hear?"

"I am the bailiff of the town," said Mr. Tinman.

"You're going to Court, I'm told."

"The appointment," replied Mr. Tinman, "will soon be made. I have not yet an appointed day."

On the great highroad of life there is Expectation, and there is Attainment, and also there is Envy. Mr. Tinman's posture stood for Attainment shadowing Expectation, and sunning itself in the glass of

Envy, as he spoke of the appointed day. It was involuntary, and naturally evanescent, a momentary view of the spirit.

He unbent, and begged to be excused for the present, that he might go and apprise his sister of guests coming.

"All right. I daresay we shall see, enough of one another," said Van Diemen. And almost before the creak of Tinman's heels was deadened on the road outside the shop, he put the funny question to Crickledon, "Do you box?"

"I make 'em," Crickledon replied.

"Because I should like to have a go in at something, my friend."

Van Diemen stretched and yawned.

Crickledon recommended the taking of a walk.

"I think I will," said the other, and turned back abruptly. "How long do you work in the day?"

"Generally, all the hours of light," Crickledon replied; "and always up to supper-time."

"You're healthy and happy?"

"Nothing to complain of."

"Good appetite?"

"Pretty regular."

"You never take a holiday?"

"Except Sundays."

"You'd like to be working then?"

"I won't say that."

"But you're glad to be up Monday morning?"

"It feels cheerfuller in the shop."

"And carpentering's your joy?"

"I think I may say so."

Van Diemen slapped his thigh. "There's life in Old England yet!"

Crickledon eyed him as he walked away to the beach to look for his daughter, and conceived that there was a touch of the soldier in him.

CHAPTER IV

Annette Smith's delight in her native England made her see beauty and kindness everywhere around her; it put a halo about the house on the beach, and thrilled her at Tinman's table when she heard the thunder of the waves hard by. She fancied it had been a most agreeable dinner to her father and Mr. Herbert Fellingham — especially to the latter, who had laughed very much; and she was astonished to hear them at breakfast both complaining of their evening. In answer to which, she exclaimed, "Oh, I think the situation of the house is so romantic!"

"The situation of the host is exceedingly so," said Mr. Fellingham; "but
I think his wine the most unromantic liquid I have ever tasted."

"It must be that!" cried Van Diemen, puzzled by novel pains in the head.
"Old Martin woke up a little like his old self after dinner."

"He drank sparingly," said Mr. Fellingham.

"I am sure you were satirical last night," Annette said reproachfully.

"On the contrary, I told him I thought he was in a romantic situation."

"But I have had a French mademoiselle for my governess and an Oxford gentleman for my tutor; and I know you accepted French and English from Mr. Tinman and his sister that I should not have approved."

"Netty," said Van Diemen, "has had the best instruction money could procure; and if she says you were satirical, you may depend on it you were."

"Oh, in that case, of course!" Mr. Fellingham rejoined. "Who could help it?"

He thought himself warranted in giving the rein to his wicked satirical spirit, and talked lightly of the accidental character of the letter H in Tinman's pronunciation; of how, like somebody else's hat in a high wind, it descended on somebody else's head, and of how his words walked about asking one another who they were and what they were doing, danced together madly, snapping their fingers at signification; and so forth. He was flippant.

Annette glanced at her father, and dropped her eyelids.

Mr. Fellingham perceived that he was enjoined to be on his guard.

He went one step farther in his fun; upon which Van Diemen said, with a frown, "If you please!"

Nothing could withstand that.

"Hang old Mart Tinman's wine!" Van Diemen burst out in the dead pause.
"My head's a bullet. I'm in a shocking bad temper. I can hardly see. I'm bilious."

Mr. Fellingham counselled his lying down for an hour, and he went grumbling, complaining of Mart Tinman's incredulity about the towering beauty of a place in Australia called Gippsland.

Annette confided to Mr. Fellingham, as soon as they were alone, the chivalrous nature of her father in his friendships, and his indisposition to hear a satirical remark upon his old schoolmate, the moment he understood it to be satire.

Fellingham pleaded: "The man's a perfect burlesque. He's as distinctly made to be laughed at as a mask in a pantomime."

"Papa will not think so," said Annette; "and papa has been told that he is not to be laughed at as a man of business."

"Do you prize him for that?"

"I am no judge. I am too happy to be in England to be a judge of anything."

"You did not touch his wine!"

"You men attach so much importance to wine!"

"They do say that powders is a good thing after Mr. Tinman's wine," observed Mrs. Crickledon, who had come into the sitting-room to take away the breakfast things.

Mr. Fellingham gave a peal of laughter; but Mrs Crickledon bade him be hushed, for Mr. Van Diemen Smith had gone to lay down his poor aching head on his pillow. Annette ran upstairs to speak to her father about a doctor.

During her absence, Mr. Fellingham received the popular portrait of Mr. Tinman from the lips of Mrs. Crickledon. He subsequently strolled to the carpenter's shop, and endeavoured to get a confirmation of it.

"My wife talks too much," said Crickledon.

When questioned by a gentleman, however, he was naturally bound to answer to the extent of his knowledge.

"What a funny old country it is!" Mr. Fellingham said to Annette, on their walk to the beach.

She implored him not to laugh at anything English.

"I don't, I assure you," said he. "I love the country, too. But when one comes back from abroad, and plunges into their daily life, it's difficult to retain the real figure of the old country seen from outside, and one has to remember half a dozen great names to right oneself. And Englishmen are so funny! Your father comes here to see his old friend, and begins boasting of the Gippsland he has left behind. Tinman immediately brags of Helvellyn, and they fling mountains at one another till, on their first evening together, there's earthquake and rupture— they were nearly at fisticuffs at one time."

"Oh! surely no," said Annette. "I did not hear them. They were good friends when you came to the drawingroom. Perhaps the wine did affect poor papa, if it was bad wine. I wish men would never drink any. How much happier they would be."

"But then there would cease to be social meetings in England. What should we do?"

"I know that is a sneer; and you were nearly as enthusiastic as I was on board the vessel," Annette said, sadly.

"Quite true. I was. But see what quaint creatures we have about us! Tinman practicing in his Court suit before the chiwal-glass! And that good fellow, the carpenter, Crickledon, who has lived with the sea fronting him all his life, and has never been in a boat, and he confesses he has only once gone inland, and has never seen an acorn!"

"I wish I could see one — of a real English oak," said Annette.

"And after being in England a few months you will be sighing for the Continent."

"Never!"

"You think you will be quite contented here?"

"I am sure I shall be. May papa and I never be exiles again! I did not feel it when I was three years old, going out to Australia; but it would be like death to me now. Oh!" Annette shivered, as with the exile's chill.

"On my honour," said Mr. Fellingham, as softly as he could with the wind in his teeth, "I love the old country ten times more from your love of it."

"That is not how I want England to be loved," returned Annette.

"The love is in your hands."

She seemed indifferent on hearing it.

He should have seen that the way to woo her was to humour her prepossession by another passion. He could feel that it ennobled her in the abstract, but a latent spite at Tinman on account of his wine, to which he continued angrily to attribute as unwonted dizziness of the head and slight irascibility, made him urgent in his desire that she should separate herself from Tinman and his sister by the sharp division of derision.

Annette declined to laugh at the most risible caricatures of Tinman. In her antagonism she forced her simplicity so far as to say that she did not think him absurd. And supposing Mr. Tinman to have proposed to the titled widow, Lady Ray, as she had heard, and to other ladies young and middle-aged in the neighbourhood, why should he not, if he wished to marry? If he was economical, surely he had a right to manage his own affairs. Her dread was lest Mr. Tinman and her father should quarrel over the payment for the broken chiwal-glass: that she honestly admitted, and Fellingham was so indiscreet as to roar aloud, not so very cordially.

Annette thought him unkindly satirical; and his thoughts of her reduced her to the condition of a commonplace girl with expressive eyes.

She had to return to her father. Mr. Fellingham took a walk on the springy turf along the cliffs; and "certainly she is a commonplace girl," he began by reflecting; with a side eye at the fact that his meditations were excited by Tinman's poisoning of his bile. "A girl who can't see the absurdity of Tinman must be destitute of common intelligence." After a while he sniffed the fine sharp air of mingled earth and sea delightedly, and he strode back to the town late in the afternoon, laughing at himself in scorn of his wretched susceptibility to bilious impressions, and really all but hating Tinman as the cause of his weakness—in the manner of the criminal hating the detective, perhaps. He cast it altogether on Tinman that Annette's complexion of character had become discoloured to his mind; for, in spite of the physical freshness with which he returned to her society, he was incapable of throwing off the idea of her being commonplace; and it was with regret that he acknowledged he had gained from his walk only a higher opinion of himself.

Her father was the victim of a sick headache, [Migraine—D.W.] and lay, a groaning man, on his bed, ministered to by Mrs. Crickledon chiefly. Annette had to conduct the business with Mr. Phippun and Mr. Tinman as to payment for the chiwal-glass. She was commissioned to offer half the price for the glass on her father's part; more he would not pay. Tinman and Phippun sat with her in Crickledon's cottage, and Mrs. Crickledon brought down two messages from her invalid, each positive, to the effect that he would fight with all the arms of English law rather than yield his point.

Tinman declared it to be quite out of the question that he should pay a penny. Phippun vowed that from one or the other of them he would have the money.

Annette naturally was in deep distress, and Fellingham postponed the discussion to the morrow.

Even after such a taste of Tinman as that, Annette could not be induced to join in deriding him privately. She looked pained by Mr. Fellingham's cruel jests. It was monstrous, Fellingham considered, that he should draw on himself a second reprimand from Van Diemen

Smith, while they were consulting in entire agreement upon the case of the chiwal-glass.

"I must tell you this, mister sir," said Van Diemen, "I like you, but I'll be straightforward and truthful, or I'm not worthy the name of Englishman; and I do like you, or I should n't have given you leave to come down here after us two. You must respect my friend if you care for my respect. That's it. There it is. Now you know my conditions."

"I 'm afraid I can't sign the treaty," said Fellingham.

"Here's more," said Van Diemen. "I'm a chilly man myself if I hear a laugh and think I know the aim of it. I'll meet what you like except scorn. I can't stand contempt. So I feel for another. And now you know."

"It puts a stopper on the play of fancy, and checks the throwing off of steam," Fellingham remonstrated. "I promise to do my best, but of all the men I've ever met in my life — Tinman! — the ridiculous! Pray pardon me; but the donkey and his looking-glass! The glass was misty! He — as particular about his reflection in the glass as a poet with his verses! Advance, retire, bow; and such murder of the Queen's English in the very presence! If I thought he was going to take his wine with him, I'd have him arrested for high treason."

"You've chosen, and you know what you best like," said Van Diemen, pointing his accents — by which is produced the awkward pause, the pitfall of conversation, and sometimes of amity.

Thus it happened that Mr. Herbert Fellingham journeyed back to London a day earlier than he had intended, and without saying what he meant to say.

CHAPTER V

A month later, after a night of sharp frost on the verge of the warmer days of spring, Mr. Fellingham entered Crikswich under a sky of perfect blue that was in brilliant harmony with the green downs, the white cliffs and sparkling sea, and no doubt it was the beauty before his eyes which persuaded him of his delusion in having taken Annette for a commonplace girl. He had come in a merely curious mood to discover whether she was one or not. Who but a commonplace girl would care to reside in Crikswich, he had asked himself; and now he was full sure that no commonplace girl would ever have had the idea. Exquisitely simple, she certainly was; but that may well be a distinction in a young lady whose eyes are expressive.

The sound of sawing attracted him to Crickledon's shop, and the industrious carpenter soon put him on the tide of affairs.

Crickledon pointed to the house on the beach as the place where Mr. Van
Diemen Smith and his daughter were staying.

"Dear me! and how does he look?" said Fellingham.

"Our town seems to agree with him, sir."

"Well, I must not say any more, I suppose." Fellingham checked his tongue. "How have they settled that dispute about the chiwal-glass?"

"Mr. Tinman had to give way."

"Really."

"But," Crickledon stopped work, "Mr. Tinman sold him a meadow."

"I see."

"Mr. Smith has been buying a goodish bit of ground here. They tell me he's about purchasing Elba. He has bought the Crouch. He and

Mr. Tinman are always out together. They're over at Helmstone now. They've been to London."

"Are they likely to be back to-day?"

"Certain, I should think. Mr. Tinman has to be in London to-morrow."

Crickledon looked. He was not the man to look artful, but there was a lighted corner in his look that revived Fellingham's recollections, and the latter burst out:

"The Address? I'd half forgotten it. That's not over yet? Has he been practicing much?"

"No more glasses ha' been broken."

"And how is your wife, Crickledon?"

"She's at home, sir, ready for a talk, if you've a mind to try her."

Mrs. Crickledon proved to be very ready. "That Tinman," was her theme. He had taken away her lodgers, and she knew his objects. Mr. Smith repented of leaving her, she knew, though he dared not say it in plain words. She knew Miss Smith was tired to death of constant companionship with Mrs. Cavely, Tinman's sister. She generally came once in the day just to escape from Mrs. Cavely, who would not, bless you! step into a cottager's house where she was not allowed to patronize. Fortunately Miss Smith had induced her father to get his own wine from the merchants.

"A happy resolution," said Fellingham; "and a saving one."

He heard further that Mr. Smith would take possession of the Crouch next month, and that Mrs. Cavely hung over Miss Smith like a kite.

"And that old Tinman, old enough to be her father!" said Mrs. Crickledon.

She dealt in the flashes which connect ideas. Fellingham, though a man, and an Englishman, was nervously wakeful enough to see the connection.

"They'll have to consult the young lady first, ma'am."

"If it's her father's nod she'll bow to it; now mark me," Mrs. Crickledon said, with emphasis. "She's a young lady who thinks for herself, but she takes her start from her father where it's feeling. And he's gone stone- blind over that Tinman."

While they were speaking, Annette appeared.

"I saw you," she said to Fellingham; gladly and openly, in the most commonplace manner.

"Are you going to give me a walk along the beach?" said he.

She proposed the country behind the town, and that was quite as much to his taste. But it was not a happy walk. He had decided that he admired her, and the notion of having Tinman for a rival annoyed him. He overflowed with ridicule of Tinman, and this was distressing to Annette, because not only did she see that he would not control himself before her father, but he kindled her own satirical spirit in opposition to her father's friendly sentiments toward his old schoolmate.

"Mr. Tinman has been extremely hospitable to us," she said, a little coldly.

"May I ask you, has he consented to receive instruction in deportment and pronunciation?"

Annette did not answer.

"If practice makes perfect, he must be near the mark by this time."

She continued silent.

"I dare say, in domestic life, he's as amiable as he is hospitable, and it must be a daily gratification to see him in his Court suit."

"I have not seen him in his Court suit."

"That is his coyness."

"People talk of those things."

"The common people scandalize the great, about whom they know nothing, you mean! I am sure that is true, and living in Courts one must be keenly aware of it. But what a splendid sky and-sea!"

"Is it not?"

Annette echoed his false rapture with a candour that melted him.

He was preparing to make up for lost time, when the wild waving of a parasol down a road to the right, coming from the town, caused Annette to stop and say, "I think that must be Mrs. Cavely. We ought to meet her."

Fellingham asked why.

"She is so fond of walks," Anisette replied, with a tooth on her lip

Fellingham thought she seemed fond of runs.

Mrs. Cavely joined them, breathless. "My dear! the pace you go at!" she shouted. "I saw you starting. I followed, I ran, I tore along. I feared I never should catch you. And to lose such a morning of English scenery!

"Is it not heavenly?"

"One can't say more," Fellingham observed, bowing.

"I am sure I am very glad to see you again, sir. You enjoy Crikswich?"

"Once visited, always desired, like Venice, ma'am. May I venture to inquire whether Mr. Tinman has presented his Address?"

"The day after to-morrow. The appointment is made with him," said Mrs. Cavely, more officially in manner, "for the day after to-morrow. He is excited, as you may well believe. But Mr. Smith is an immense relief to him—the very distraction he wanted. We have become one family, you know."

"Indeed, ma'am, I did not know it," said Fellingham.

The communication imparted such satiric venom to his further remarks, that Annette resolved to break her walk and dismiss him for the day.

He called at the house on the beach after the dinner-hour, to see Mr. Van Diemen Smith, when there was literally a duel between him and Tinman; for Van Diemen's contribution to the table was champagne, and that had been drunk, but Tinman's sherry remained. Tinman would insist on Fellingham's taking a glass. Fellingham parried him with a sedate gravity of irony that was painfully perceptible to Anisette. Van Diemen at last backed Tinman's hospitable intent, and, to Fellingham's astonishment, he found that he had been supposed by these two men to be bashfully retreating from a seductive offer all the time that his tricks of fence and transpiercings of one of them had been marvels of skill.

Tinman pushed the glass into his hand.

"You have spilt some," said Fellingham.

"It won't hurt the carpet," said Tinman.

"Won't it?" Fellingham gazed at the carpet, as if expecting a flame to arise.

He then related the tale of the magnanimous Alexander drinking off the potion, in scorn of the slanderer, to show faith in his friend.

"Alexander — Who was that?" said Tinman, foiled in his historical recollections by the absence of the surname.

"General Alexander," said Fellingham. "Alexander Philipson, or he declared it was Joveson; and very fond of wine. But his sherry did for him at last."

"Ah! he drank too much, then," said Tinman.

"Of his own!"

Anisette admonished the vindictive young gentleman by saying, "How long do you stay in Crikswich, Mr. Fellingham?"

He had grossly misconducted himself. But an adversary at once offensive and helpless provokes brutality. Anisette prudently avoided letting her father understand that satire was in the air; and neither he nor Tinman was conscious of it exactly: yet both shrank within themselves under the sensation of a devilish blast blowing. Fellingham accompanied them and certain jurats to London next day.

Yes, if you like: when a mayor visits Majesty, it is an important circumstance, and you are at liberty to argue at length that it means more than a desire on his part to show his writing power and his reading power: it is full of comfort the people, as an exhibition of their majesty likewise; and it is an encouragement to men to strive to become mayors, bailiffs, or prime men of any sort; but a stress in the reporting of it — the making it appear too important a circumstance — will surely breathe the intimation to a politically-minded people that satire is in the air, and however dearly they cherish the privilege of knocking at the first door of the kingdom, and walking ceremoniously in to read their writings, they will, if they are not in one of their moods for prostration, laugh. They will laugh at the report.

All the greater reason is it that we should not indulge them at such periods; and I say woe's me for any brother of the pen, and one in some esteem, who dressed the report of that presentation of the Address of congratulation by Mr. Bailiff Tinman, of Crikswich! Herbert Fellingham wreaked his personal spite on Tinman. He should have bethought him that it involved another than Tinman that is to say, an office — which the fitful beast rejoices to paw and play with contemptuously now and then, one may think, as a solace to his pride, and an indemnification for those caprices of abject worship so strongly recalling the days we see through Mr. Darwin's glasses.

He should not have written the report. It sent a titter over England. He was so unwise as to despatch a copy of the newspaper containing it to Van Diemen Smith. Van Diemen perused it with satisfaction. So did Tinman. Both of these praised the able young writer. But they handed the paper to the Coastguard Lieutenant, who asked Tinman how he liked it; and visitors were beginning to drop in to Crikswich, who made a point of asking for a sight of the chief man; and then came a comic publication, all in the Republican tone of the time, with Man's Dignity for the standpoint, and the wheezy laughter residing in old puns to back it, in eulogy of the satiric report of the famous Address of congratulation of the Bailiff of Crikswich.

"Annette," Van Diemen said to his daughter, "you'll not encourage that newspaper fellow to come down here any more. He had his warning."

CHAPTER VI

One of the most difficult lessons for spirited young men to learn is, that good jokes are not always good policy. They have to be paid for, like good dinners, though dinner and joke shall seem to have been at somebody else's expense. Young Fellingham was treated rudely by Van Diemen Smith, and with some cold reserve by Annette: in consequence of which he thought her more than ever commonplace. He wrote her a letter of playful remonstrance, followed by one that appealed to her sentiments.

But she replied to neither of them. So his visits to Crikswich came to an end.

Shall a girl who has no appreciation of fun affect us? Her expressive eyes, and her quaint simplicity, and her enthusiasm for England, haunted Mr. Fellingham; being conjured up by contrast with what he met about him. But shall a girl who would impose upon us the task of holding in our laughter at Tinman be much regretted? There could be no companionship between us, Fellingham thought.

On an excursion to the English Lakes he saw the name of Van Diemen Smith in a visitors' book, and changed his ideas on the subject of companionship. Among mountains, or on the sea, or reading history, Annette was one in a thousand. He happened to be at a public ball at Helmstone in the Winter season, and who but Annette herself came whirling before him on the arm of an officer! Fellingham did not miss his chance of talking to her. She greeted him gaily, and speaking with the excitement of the dance upon her, appeared a stranger to the serious emotions he was willing to cherish. She had been to the Lakes and to Scotland. Next summer she was going to Wales. All her experiences were delicious. She was insatiable, but satisfied.

"I wish I had been with you," said Fellingham.

"I wish you had," said she.

Mrs. Cavely was her chaperon at the ball, and he was not permitted to enjoy a lengthened conversation sitting with Annette. What was he to think of a girl who could be submissive to Mrs. Cavely, and danced with any number of officers, and had no idea save of running incessantly over England in the pursuit of pleasure? Her tone of saying, "I wish you had," was that of the most ordinary of wishes, distinctly, if not designedly different from his own melodious depth.

She granted him one waltz, and he talked of her father and his whimsical vagrancies and feeling he had a positive liking for Van Diemen, and he sagaciously said so.

Annette's eyes brightened. "Then why do you never go to see him? He has bought Elba. We move into the Hall after Christmas. We are at the Crouch at present. Papa will be sure to make you welcome. Do you not know that he never forgets a friend or breaks a friendship?"

"I do, and I love him for it," said Fellingham.

If he was not greatly mistaken a gentle pressure on the fingers of his left hand rewarded him.

This determined him. It should here be observed that he was by birth the superior of Annette's parentage, and such is the sentiment of a better blood that the flattery of her warm touch was needed for him to overlook the distinction.

Two of his visits to Crikswich resulted simply in interviews and conversations with Mrs. Crickledon. Van Diemen and his daughter were in London with Tinman and Mrs. Cavely, purchasing furniture for Elba Hall. Mrs. Crickledon had no scruple in saying, that Mrs. Cavely meant her brother to inhabit the Hall, though Mr. Smith had outbid him in the purchase. According to her, Tinman and Mr. Smith had their differences; for Mr. Smith was a very outspoken gentleman, and had been known to call Tinman names that no man of spirit would bear if he was not scheming.

Fellingham returned to London, where he roamed the streets famous for furniture warehouses, in the vain hope of encountering the new owner of Elba.

Failing in this endeavour, he wrote a love-letter to Annette.

It was her first. She had liked him. Her manner of thinking she might love him was through the reflection that no one stood in the way. The letter opened a world to her, broader than Great Britain.

Fellingham begged her, if she thought favourably of him, to prepare her father for the purport of his visit. If otherwise, she was to interdict the visit with as little delay as possible and cut him adrift.

A decided line of conduct was imperative. Yet you have seen that she was not in love. She was only not unwilling to be in love. And Fellingham was just a trifle warmed. Now mark what events will do to light the fires.

Van Diemen and Tinman, old chums re-united, and both successful in life, had nevertheless, as Mrs. Crickledon said, their differences. They commenced with an opposition to Tinman's views regarding the expenditure of town moneys. Tinman was ever for devoting them to the patriotic defence of "our shores;" whereas Van Diemen, pointing in detestation of the town sewerage reeking across the common under the beach, loudly called on him to preserve our lives, by way of commencement. Then Van Diemen precipitately purchased Elba at a high valuation, and Tinman had expected by waiting to buy it at his own valuation, and sell it out of friendly consideration to his friend afterwards, for a friendly consideration. Van Diemen had joined the hunt. Tinman could not mount a horse. They had not quarrelled, but they had snapped about these and other affairs. Van Diemen fancied Tinman was jealous of his wealth. Tinman shrewdly suspected Van Diemen to be contemptuous of his dignity. He suffered a loss in a loan of money; and instead of pitying him, Van Diemen had laughed him to scorn for expecting security for investments at ten per cent. The bitterness of the pinch to Tinman made him frightfully sensitive to strictures on his discretion. In his anguish he told his sister he was ruined, and she advised him to marry before the crash. She was aware that he exaggerated, but she repeated her advice. She went so far as to name the person. This is known, because she was overheard by her housemaid, a gossip of Mrs. Crickledon's, the subsequently famous "Little Jane."

Now, Annette had shyly intimated to her father the nature of Herbert Fellingham's letter, at the same time professing a perfect readiness to submit to his directions; and her father's perplexity was very great, for Annette had rather fervently dramatized the young man's words at the ball at Helmstone, which had pleasantly tickled him, and, besides, he liked the young man. On the other hand, he did not at all like the prospect of losing his daughter; and he would have desired her to be a lady of title. He hinted at her right to claim a high position. Annette shrank from the prospect, saying, "Never let me marry one who might be ashamed of my father!"

"I shouldn't stomach that," said Van Diemen, more disposed in favour of the present suitor.

Annette was now in a tremor. She had a lover; he was coming. And if he did not come, did it matter? Not so very much, except to her pride. And if he did, what was she to say to him? She felt like an actress who may in a few minutes be called on the stage, without knowing her part. This was painfully unlike love, and the poor girl feared it would be her conscientious duty to dismiss him—most gently, of course; and perhaps, should he be impetuous and picturesque, relent enough to let him hope, and so bring about a happy postponement of the question. Her father had been to a neighbouring town on business with Mr. Tinman. He knocked at her door at midnight; and she, in dread of she knew not what—chiefly that the Hour of the Scene had somehow struck—stepped out to him trembling. He was alone. She thought herself the most childish of mortals in supposing that she could have been summoned at midnight to declare her sentiments, and hardly noticed his gloomy depression. He asked her to give him five minutes; then asked her for a kiss, and told her to go to bed and sleep. But Annette had seen that a great present affliction was on him, and she would not be sent to sleep. She promised to listen patiently, to bear anything, to be brave. "Is it bad news from home?" she said, speaking of the old home where she had not left her heart, and where his money was invested.

"It's this, my dear Netty," said Van Diemen, suffering her to lead him into her sitting-room; "we shall have to leave the shores of England."

"Then we are ruined."

"We're not; the rascal can't do that. We might be off to the Continent, or we might go to America; we've money. But we can't stay here. I'll not live at any man's mercy."

"The Continent! America!" exclaimed the enthusiast for England. "Oh, papa, you love living in England so!"

"Not so much as all that, my dear. You do, that I know. But I don't see how it's to be managed. Mart Tinman and I have been at tooth and claw to-day and half the night; and he has thrown off the mask, or he's dashed something from my sight, I don't know which. I knocked him down."

"Papa!"

"I picked him up."

"Oh," cried Annette, "has Mr. Tinman been hurt?"

"He called me a Deserter!"

Anisette shuddered.

She did not know what this thing was, but the name of it opened a cabinet of horrors, and she touched her father timidly, to assure him of her constant love, and a little to reassure herself of his substantial identity.

"And I am one," Van Diemen made the confession at the pitch of his voice. "I am a Deserter; I'm liable to be branded on the back. And it's in Mart Tinman's power to have me marched away to-morrow morning in the sight of Crikswich, and all I can say for myself, as a man and a Briton, is, I did not desert before the enemy. That I swear I never would have done. Death, if death's in front; but your poor mother was a handsome woman, my child, and there—I could not go on living in barracks and leaving her unprotected. I can't tell a young woman the tale. A hundred pounds came on me for a legacy, as plump in my hands out of open heaven, and your poor mother and I saw our chance; we consulted, and we determined to risk it, and I got on board with her and you, and over the seas we went, first to shipwreck, ultimately to fortune."

Van Diemen laughed miserably. "They noticed in the hunting-field here I had a soldier-like seat. A soldier-like seat it'll be, with a brand on it. I sha'n't be asked to take a soldier-like seat at any of their tables again. I may at Mart Tinman's, out of pity, after I've undergone my punishment. There's a year still to run out of the twenty of my term of service due. He knows it; he's been reckoning; he has me. But the worst cat-o'-nine-tails for me is the disgrace. To have myself pointed at, 'There goes the Deserter' He was a private in the Carbineers, and he deserted.' No one'll say, 'Ay, but he clung to the idea of his old schoolmate when abroad, and came back loving him, and trusted him, and was deceived."

Van Diemen produced a spasmodic cough with a blow on his chest. Anisette was weeping.

"There, now go to bed," said he. "I wish you might have known no more than you did of our flight when I got you on board the ship with your poor mother; but you're a young woman now, and you must help me to think of another cut and run, and what baggage we can scrape together in a jiffy, for I won't live here at Mart Tinman's mercy."

Drying her eyes to weep again, Annette said, when she could speak: "Will nothing quiet him? I was going to bother you with all sorts of silly questions, poor dear papa; but I see I can understand if I try. Will nothing—Is he so very angry? Can we not do something to pacify him? He is fond of money. He—oh, the thought of leaving England! Papa, it will kill you; you set your whole heart on England. We could—I could—could I not, do you not think?—step between you as a peacemaker. Mr. Tinman is always very courteous to me."

At these words of Annette's, Van Diemen burst into a short snap of savage laughter. "But that's far away in the background, Mr. Mart Tinman!" he said. "You stick to your game, I know that; but you'll find me flown, though I leave a name to stink like your common behind me. And," he added, as a chill reminder, "that name the name of my benefactor. Poor old Van Diemen! He thought it a safe bequest to make."

"It was; it is! We will stay; we will not be exiled," said Annette. "I will do anything. What was the quarrel about, papa?"

"The fact is, my dear, I just wanted to show him—and take down his pride—I'm by my Australian education a shrewder hand than his old country. I bought the house on the beach while he was chaffering, and then I sold it him at a rise when the town was looking up—only to make him see. Then he burst up about something I said of Australia. I will have the common clean. Let him live at the Crouch as my tenant if he finds the house on the beach in danger."

"Papa, I am sure," Annette repeated — "sure I have influence with Mr. Tinman."

"There are those lips of yours shutting tight," said her father. "Just listen, and they make a big O. The donkey! He owns you've got influence, and he offers he'll be silent if you'll pledge your word to marry him. I'm not sure he didn't say, within the year. I told him to look sharp not to be knocked down again. Mart Tinman for my son-in-law! That's an upside down of my expectations, as good as being at the antipodes without a second voyage back! I let him know you were engaged."

Annette gazed at her father open-mouthed, as he had predicted; now with a little chilly dimple at one corner of the mouth, now at another — as a breeze curves the leaden winter lake here and there. She could not get his meaning into her sight, and she sought, by looking hard, to understand it better; much as when some solitary maiden lady, passing into her bedchamber in the hours of darkness, beholds — tradition telling us she has absolutely beheld foot of burglar under bed; and lo! she stares, and, cunningly to moderate her horror, doubts, yet cannot but believe that there is a leg, and a trunk, and a head, and two terrible arms, bearing pistols, to follow. Sick, she palpitates; she compresses her trepidation; she coughs, perchance she sings a bar or two of an aria. Glancing down again, thrice horrible to her is it to discover that there is no foot! For had it remained, it might have been imagined a harmless, empty boot. But the withdrawal has a deadly significance of animal life . . . .

In like manner our stricken Annette perceived the object; so did she gradually apprehend the fact of her being asked for Tinman's bride, and she could not think it credible. She half scented, she devised her plan of escape from another single mention of it. But on her father's remarking, with a shuffle, frightened by her countenance, "Don't listen to what I said, Netty. I won't paint him blacker than he is" — then Annette was sure she had been proposed for by Mr. Tinman, and she fancied her father might have revolved it in his mind that there was this means of keeping Tinman silent, silent for ever, in his own interests.

"It was not true, when you told Mr. Tinman I was engaged, papa," she said.

"No, I know that. Mart Tinman only half-kind of hinted. Come, I say! Where's the unmarried man wouldn't like to have a girl like you, Netty! They say he's been rejected all round a circuit of fifteen miles; and he's not bad-looking, neither — he looks fresh and fair. But I thought it as well to let him know he might get me at a disadvantage, but he couldn't you. Now, don't think about it, my love."

"Not if it is not necessary, papa," said Annette; and employed her familiar sweetness in persuading him to go to bed, as though he were the afflicted one requiring to be petted.

CHAPTER VII

Round under the cliffs by the sea, facing South, are warm seats in winter. The sun that shines there on a day of frost wraps you as in a mantle. Here it was that Mr. Herbert Fellingham found Annette, a chalk- block for her chair, and a mound of chalk-rubble defending her from the keen-tipped breath of the east, now and then shadowing the smooth blue water, faintly, like reflections of a flight of gulls.

Infants are said to have their ideas, and why not young ladies? Those who write of their perplexities in descriptions comical in their length are unkind to them, by making them appear the simplest of the creatures of fiction; and most of us, I am sure, would incline to believe in them if they were only some bit more lightly touched. Those troubled sentiments of our young lady of the comfortable classes are quite worthy of mention. Her poor little eye poring as little fishlike as possible upon the intricate, which she takes for the infinite, has its place in our history, nor should we any of us miss the pathos of it were it not that so large a space is claimed for the exposure. As it is, one has almost to fight a battle to persuade the world that she has downright thoughts and feelings, and really a superhuman delicacy is required in presenting her that she may be credible. Even then — so much being accomplished the thousands accustomed to chapters of her when she is in the situation of Annette will be disappointed by short sentences, just as of old the Continental eater of oysters would have been offended at the offer of an exchange of two live for two dozen dead ones. Annette was in the grand crucial position of English imaginative prose. I recognize it, and that to this the streamlets flow, thence pours the flood. But what was the plain truth? She had brought herself to think she ought to sacrifice herself to Tinman, and her evasions with Herbert, manifested in tricks of coldness alternating with tones of regret, ended, as they had commenced, in a mysterious half-sullenness. She had hardly a word to say. Let me step in again to observe that she had at the moment no pointed intention of marrying Tinman. To her mind the circumstances compelled her to embark on the idea of doing so, and she saw the extremity in an extreme distance, as those who are taking voyages may see death by drowning. Still she had embarked.

"At all events, I have your word for it that you don't dislike me?" said Herbert.

"Oh! no," she sighed. She liked him as emigrants the land they are leaving.

"And you have not promised your hand?"

"No," she said, but sighed in thinking that if she could be induced to promise it, there would not be a word of leaving England.

"Then, as you are not engaged, and don't hate me, I have a chance?" he said, in the semi-wailful interrogative of an organ making a mere windy conclusion.

Ocean sent up a tiny wave at their feet.

"A day like this in winter is rarer than a summer day," Herbert resumed encouragingly.

Annette was replying, "People abuse our climate—"

But the thought of having to go out away from this climate in the darkness of exile, with her father to suffer under it worse than herself, overwhelmed her, and fetched the reality of her sorrow in the form of Tinman swimming before her soul with the velocity of a telegraph-pole to the window of the flying train. It was past as soon as seen, but it gave her a desperate sensation of speed.

She began to feel that this was life in earnest.

And Herbert should have been more resolute, fierier. She needed a strong will.

But he was not on the rapids of the masterful passion. For though going at a certain pace, it was by his own impulsion; and I am afraid I must, with many apologies, compare him to the skater—to the skater on easy, slippery ice, be it understood; but he could perform gyrations as he went, and he rather sailed along than dashed; he was careful of his figuring. Some lovers, right honest lovers, never get beyond this quaint skating-stage; and some ladies, a right goodly number in a foggy climate, deceived by their occasional runs ahead, take them for vessels on the very torrent of love. Let them take them, and let the race continue. Only we perceive that they are skating; they are careering over a smooth icy floor, and they can stop at a signal, with just half-a-yard of grating on the heel at the outside. Ice, and not fire nor falling water, has been their medium of progression.

Whether a man should unveil his own sex is quite another question. If we are detected, not solely are we done for, but our love-tales too. However, there is not much ground for anxiety on that head. Each member of the other party is blind on her own account.

To Annette the figuring of Herbert was graceful, but it did not catch her up and carry her; it hardly touched her: He spoke well enough to make her sorry for him, and not warmly enough to make her forget her sorrow for herself.

Herbert could obtain no explanation of the singularity of her conduct from Annette, and he went straight to her father, who was nearly as inexplicable for a time. At last he said:

"If you are ready to quit the country with us, you may have my consent."

"Why quit the country?" Herbert asked, in natural amazement.

Van Diemen declined to tell him.

But seeing the young man look stupefied and wretched he took a turn about the room, and said: "I have n't robbed," and after more turns, "I have n't murdered." He growled in his menagerie trot within the four walls. "But I'm, in a man's power. Will that satisfy you? You'll tell me, because I'm rich, to snap my fingers. I can't. I've got feelings. I'm in his power to hurt me and disgrace me. It's the disgrace—to my disgrace I say it—I dread most. You'd be up to my reason if you had ever served in a regiment. I mean, discipline—if ever you'd known discipline—in the police if you like—anything—anywhere where there's what we used to call spiny de cor. I mean, at school. And I'm," said Van Diemen, "a rank idiot double D. dolt, and flat as a pancake, and transparent as a pane of glass. You see through me. Anybody could. I can't talk of my botheration without betraying myself. What good am I among you sharp fellows in England?"

Language of this kind, by virtue of its unintelligibility, set Mr. Herbert Fellingham's acute speculations at work. He was obliged to lean on Van Diemen's assertion, that he had not robbed and had not murdered, to be comforted by the belief that he was not once a notorious bushranger, or a defaulting manager of mines, or any other thing that is naughtily Australian and kangarooly.

He sat at the dinner-table at Elba, eating like the rest of mankind, and looking like a starved beggarman all the while.

Annette, in pity of his bewilderment, would have had her father take him into their confidence. She suggested it covertly, and next she spoke of it to him as a prudent measure, seeing that Mr. Fellingham might find out his exact degree of liability. Van Diemen shouted; he betrayed himself in his weakness as she could not have imagined him. He was ready to go, he said — go on the spot, give up Elba, fly from Old England: what he could not do was to let his countrymen know what he was, and live among them afterwards. He declared that the fact had eternally been present to his mind, devouring him; and Annette remembered his kindness to the artillerymen posted along the shore westward of Crikswich, though she could recall no sign of remorse. Van Diemen said: "We have to do with Martin Tinman; that's one who has a hold on me, and one's enough. Leak out my secret to a second fellow, you double my risks." He would not be taught to see how the second might counteract the first. The singularity of the action of his character on her position was, that though she knew not a soul to whom she could unburden her wretchedness, and stood far more isolated than in her Australian home, fever and chill struck her blood in contemplation of the necessity of quitting England.

Deep, then, was her gratitude to dear good Mrs. Cavely for stepping in to mediate between her father and Mr. Tinman. And well might she be amazed to hear the origin of their recent dispute.

"It was," Mrs. Cavely said, "that Gippsland."

Annette cried: "What?"

"That Gippsland of yours, my dear. Your father will praise Gippsland whenever my Martin asks him to admire the beauties of our neighbourhood. Many a time has Martin come home to me complaining of it. We have no doubt on earth that Gippsland is a very fine place; but my brother has his idea's of dignity, you must know, and I only wish he had been more used to contradiction, you may believe me. He is a lamb by nature. And, as he says, 'Why underrate one's own country?' He cannot bear to hear boasting. Well! I put it to you, dear Annette, is he so unimportant a person? He asks to be respected, and especially by his dearest friend. From that to blows! It's the way with men. They begin about trifles, they drink, they quarrel, and one does what he is sorry for, and one says more than he means. All my Martin desires is to shake your dear father's hand, forgive and forget. To win your esteem, darling Annette, he would humble himself in the dust. Will you not help me to bring these two dear old friends together once more? It is unreasonable of your dear papa to go on boasting of Gippsland if he is so fond of England, now is it not? My brother is the offended party in the eye of the law. That is quite certain. Do you suppose he dreams of taking advantage of it? He is waiting at home to be told he may call on your father. Rank, dignity, wounded feelings, is nothing to him in comparison with friendship."

Annette thought of the blow which had felled him, and spoke the truth of her heart in saying, "He is very generous."

"You understand him." Mrs. Cavely pressed her hand. "We will both go to your dear father. He may," she added, not without a gleam of feminine archness, "praise Gippsland above the Himalayas to me. What my Martin so much objected to was, the speaking of Gippsland at all when there was mention of our Lake scenery. As for me, I know how men love to boast of things nobody else has seen."

The two ladies went in company to Van Diemen, who allowed himself to be melted. He was reserved nevertheless. His reception of Mr. Tinman displeased his daughter. Annette attached the blackest importance to a blow of the fist. In her mind it blazed fiendlike, and the man who forgave it rose a step or two on the sublime. Especially did he do so considering that he had it in his power to dismiss her father and herself from bright beaming England before she had looked on all the cathedrals and churches, the sea-shores and spots named in printed poetry, to say nothing of the nobility.

"Papa, you were not so kind to Mr. Tinman as I could have hoped," said Annette.

"Mart Tinman has me at his mercy, and he'll make me know it," her father returned gloomily. "He may let me off with the Commander-in-chief. He'll blast my reputation some day, though. I shall be hanging my head in society, through him."

Van Diemen imitated the disconsolate appearance of a gallows body, in one of those rapid flashes of spontaneous veri-similitude which spring of an inborn horror painting itself on the outside.

"A Deserter!" he moaned.

He succeeded in impressing the terrible nature of the stigma upon Annette's imagination.

The guest at Elba was busy in adding up the sum of his own impressions, and dividing it by this and that new circumstance; for he was totally in the dark. He was attracted by the mysterious interview of Mrs. Cavely and Annette. Tinman's calling and departing set him upon new calculations. Annette grew cold and visibly distressed by her consciousness of it.

She endeavoured to account for this variation of mood. "We have been invited to dine at the house on the beach to-morrow. I would not have accepted, but papa . . . we seemed to think it a duty. Of course the invitation extends to you. We fancy you do not greatly enjoy dining there. The table will be laid for you here, if you prefer."

Herbert preferred to try the skill of Mrs. Crickledon.

Now, for positive penetration the head prepossessed by a suspicion is unmatched; for where there is no daylight; this one at least goes about with a lantern. Herbert begged Mrs. Crickledon to cook a dinner for him, and then to give the right colour to his absence from the table of Mr. Tinman, he started for a winter day's walk over the downs as sharpening a business as any young fellow, blunt or keen, may undertake; excellent for men of the pen, whether they be creative, and produce, or slaughtering, and review; good, then, for the silly sheep of letters and the butchers. He sat down to Mrs. Crickledon's table at half-past six. She was, as she had previously informed him, a forty-pound-a-year cook at the period of her courting by Crickledon. That zealous and devoted husband had made his first excursion inland to drop over the downs to the great house, and fetch her away as his bride, on the death of her master, Sir Alfred Pooney, who never would have parted with her in life; and every day of that man's life he dirtied thirteen plates at dinner, nor more, nor less, but exactly that number, as if he believed there was luck in it. And as Crickledon said, it was odd. But it was always a pleasure to cook for him. Mrs. Crickledon could not abide cooking for a mean eater. And when Crickledon said he had never seen an acorn, he might have seen one had he looked about him in the great park, under the oaks, on the day when he came to be married.

"Then it's a standing compliment to you, Mrs. Crickledon, that he did not," said Herbert.

He remarked with the sententiousness of enforced philosophy, that no wine was better than bad wine.

Mrs. Crickledon spoke of a bottle left by her summer lodgers, who had indeed left two, calling the wine invalid's wine; and she and her husband had opened one on the anniversary of their marriage day in October. It had the taste of doctor's shop, they both agreed; and as no friend of theirs could be tempted beyond a sip, they were advised, because it was called a tonic, to mix it with the pig-wash, so that it should not be entirely lost, but benefit the constitution of the pig. Herbert sipped at the remaining bottle, and finding himself in the superior society of an old Manzanilla, refilled his glass.

"Nothing I knows of proves the difference between gentlefolks and poor persons as tastes in wine," said Mrs. Crickledon, admiring him as she brought in a dish of cutlets, — with Sir Alfred Pooney's favourite sauce Soubise, wherein rightly onion should be delicate as the idea of love in maidens' thoughts, albeit constituting the element of flavour. Something of such a dictum Sir Alfred Pooney had imparted to his cook, and she repeated it with the fresh elegance of, such sweet sayings when transfused through the native mind:

"He said, I like as it was what you would call a young gal's blush at a kiss round a corner."

The epicurean baronet had the habit of talking in that way.

Herbert drank to his memory. He was well-filled; he had no work to do, and he was exuberant in spirits, as Mrs. Crickledon knew her countrymen should and would be under those conditions. And suddenly he drew his hand across a forehead so wrinkled and dark, that Mrs. Crickledon exclaimed, "Heart or stomach?"

"Oh, no," said he. "I'm sound enough in both, I hope."

That old Tinman's up to one of his games," she observed.

"Do you think so?"

"He's circumventing Miss Annette Smith."

"Pooh! Crickledon. A man of his age can't be seriously thinking of proposing for a young lady."

He's a well-kept man. He's never racketed. He had n't the rackets in him. And she may n't care for him. But we hear things drop."

"What things have you heard drop, Crickledon? In a profound silence you may hear pins; in a hubbub you may hear cannon-balls. But I never believe in eavesdropping gossip."

"He was heard to say to Mr. Smith," Crickledon pursued, and she lowered her voice, "he was heard to say, it was when they were quarreling over that chiwal, and they went at one another pretty hard before Mr. Smith beat him and he sold Mr. Smith that meadow; he was heard to say, there was worse than transportation for Mr. Smith if he but lifted his finger. They Tinmans have awful tempers. His old mother died malignant, though she was a saving woman, and never owed a penny to a Christian a hour longer than it took to pay the money. And old Tinman's just such another."

"Transportation!" Herbert ejaculated, "that's sheer nonsense, Crickledon.
I'm sure your husband would tell you so."

"It was my husband brought me the words," Mrs. Crickledon rejoined with some triumph. "He did tell me, I own, to keep it shut: but my speaking to you, a friend of Mr. Smith's, won't do no harm. He heard them under the battery, over that chiwal glass: 'And you shall pay,' says Mr. Smith, and 'I sha'n't,' says old Tinman. Mr. Smith said he would have it if he had to squeeze a deathbed confession from a sinner. Then old Tinman fires out, 'You!' he says, 'you' and he stammered. 'Mr. Smith,' my husband said and you never saw a man so shocked as my husband at being obliged to hear them at one another Mr. Smith used the word damn. 'You may laugh, sir.'"

"You say it so capitally, Crickledon."

"And then old Tinman said, 'And a D. to you; and if I lift my finger, it's Big D. on your back."

"And what did Mr. Smith say, then?"

"He said, like a man shot, my husband says he said, 'My God!'"

Herbert Fellingham jumped away from the table.

"You tell me, Crickledon, your husband actually heard that — just those words? — the tones?"

"My husband says he heard him say, 'My God!' just like a poor man shot or stabbed. You may speak to Crickledon, if you speaks to him alone, sir. I say you ought to know. For I've noticed Mr. Smith since that day has never looked to me the same easy-minded happy gentleman he was when we first knew him. He would have had me go to cook for him at Elba, but Crickledon thought I'd better be independent, and Mr. Smith said to me, 'Perhaps you're right, Crickledon, for who knows how long I may be among you?'"

Herbert took the solace of tobacco in Crickledon's shop. Thence, with the story confirmed to him, he sauntered toward the house on the beach.

CHAPTER VIII

The moon was over sea. Coasting vessels that had run into the bay for shelter from the North wind lay with their shadows thrown shoreward on the cold smooth water, almost to the verge of the beach, where there was neither breath nor sound of wind, only the lisp at the pebbles.

Mrs. Crickledon's dinner and the state of his heart made young Fellingham indifferent to a wintry atmosphere. It sufficed him that the night was fair. He stretched himself on the shingle, thinking of the Manzanilla, and Annette, and the fine flavour given to tobacco by a dry still air in moonlight—thinking of his work, too, in the background, as far as mental lassitude would allow of it. The idea of taking Annette to see his first play at the theatre when it should be performed—was very soothing. The beach rather looked like a stage, and the sea like a ghostly audience, with, if you will, the broadside bulks of black sailing craft at anchor for representatives of the newspaper piers. Annette was a nice girl; if a little commonplace and low-born, yet sweet. What a subject he could make of her father! "The Deserter" offered a new complication. Fellingham rapidly sketched it in fancy—Van Diemen, as a Member of the Parliament of Great Britain, led away from the House of Commons to be branded on the bank! What a magnificent fall! We have so few intensely dramatic positions in English real life that the meditative author grew enamoured of this one, and laughed out a royal "Ha!" like a monarch reviewing his well-appointed soldiery.

"There you are," said Van Diemen's voice; "I smelt your pipe. You're a rum fellow, to belying out on the beach on a cold night. Lord! I don't like you the worse for it. Twas for the romance of the moon in my young days."

"Where is Annette?" said Fellingham, jumping to his feet.

"My daughter? She's taking leave of her intended."

"What's that?" Fellingham gasped. "Good heavens, Mr. Smith, what do you mean?"

"Pick up your pipe, my lad. Girls choose as they please, I suppose"

"Her intended, did you say, sir? What can that mean?"

"My dear good young fellow, don't make a fuss. We're all going to stay here, and very glad to see you from time to time. The fact is, I oughtn't to have quarrelled with Mart Tinman as I've done; I'm too peppery by nature. The fact is, I struck him, and he forgave it. I could n't have done that myself. And I believe I'm in for a headache to-morrow; upon my soul, I do. Mart Tinman would champagne us; but, poor old boy, I struck him, and I couldn't make amends — didn't see my way; and we joined hands over the glass — to the deuce with the glass! — and the end of it is, Netty — she did n't propose it, but as I'm in his — I say, as I had struck him, she — it was rather solemn, if you had seen us — she burst into tears, and there was Mrs. Cavely, and old Mart, and me as big a fool — if I'm not a villain!"

Fellingham perceived a more than common effect of Tin man's wine. He touched Van Diemen on the shoulder. "May I beg to hear exactly what has happened?"

"Upon my soul, we're all going to live comfortably in Old England, and no more quarreling and decamping," was the stupid rejoinder. "Except that I did n't exactly — I think you said I exactly'? — I did n't bargain for old Mart as my — but he's a sound man; Mart's my junior; he's rich. He's eco . . . he's eco . . . you know — my Lord! where's my brains? — but he's upright — 'nomical!"

"An economical man," said Fellingham, with sedate impatience.

"My dear sir, I'm heartily obliged to you for your assistance," returned Van Diemen. "Here she is."

Annette had come out of the gate in the flint wall. She started slightly on seeing Herbert, whom she had taken for a coastguard, she said. He bowed. He kept his head bent, peering at her intrusively.

"It's the air on champagne," Van Diemen said, calling on his lungs to clear themselves and right him. "I was n't a bit queer in the house."

"The air on Tinman's champagne!" said Fellingham.

"It must be like the contact of two hostile chemical elements."

Annette walked faster.

They descended from the shingle to the scant-bladed grass-sweep running round the salted town-refuse on toward Elba. Van Diemen sniffed, ejaculating, "I'll be best man with Mart Tinman about this business! You'll stop with us, Mr. — — what's your Christian name? Stop with us as long as you like. Old friends for me! The joke of it is that Nelson was my man, and yet I went and enlisted in the cavalry. If you talk of chemical substances, old Mart Tinman was a sneak who never cared a dump for his country; and I'm not to speak a single sybbarel about that..... over there . . . Australia . . . Gippsland! So down he went, clean over. Very sorry for what we have done. Contrite. Penitent."

"Now we feel the wind a little," said Annette.

Fellingham murmured, "Allow me; your shawl is flying loose."

He laid his hands on her arms, and, pressing her in a tremble, said, "One sign! It's not true? A word! Do you hate me?"

"Thank you very much, but I am not cold," she replied and linked herself to her father.

Van Diemen immediately shouted, "For we are jolly boys! for we are jolly boys! It's the air on the champagne. And hang me," said he, as they entered the grounds of Elba, "if I don't walk over my property."

Annette interposed; she stood like a reed in his way.

"No! my Lord! I'll see what I sold you for!" he cried. "I'm an owner of the soil of Old England, and care no more for the title of squire than Napoleon Bonaparty. But I'll tell you what, Mr. Hubbard: your mother was never so astonished at her dog as old Van Diemen would be to hear himself called squire in Old England. And a convict he was, for he did wrong once, but he worked his redemption. And the smell of my own property makes me feel my legs again. And I'll tell you what, Mr. Hubbard, as Netty calls you when she speaks of you in private: Mart Tinman's ideas of wine are pretty much like his ideas of healthy smells, and when I'm bailiff of Crikswich, mind, he'll find two to one against him in our town council. I love my country, but hang me if I don't purify it —"

Saying this, with the excitement of a high resolve a upon him, Van Diemen bored through a shrubbery-brake, and Fellingham said to Annette:

"Have I lost you?"

"I belong to my father," said she, contracting and disengaging her feminine garments to step after him in the cold silver-spotted dusk of the winter woods.

Van Diemen came out on a fish-pond.

"Here you are, young ones!" he said to the pair. "This way, Fellowman. I'm clearer now, and it's my belief I've been talking nonsense. I'm puffed up with money, and have n't the heart I once had. I say, Fellowman, Fellowbird, Hubbard—what's your right name?—fancy an old carp fished out of that pond and flung into the sea. That's exile! And if the girl don't mind, what does it matter?"

"Mr. Herbert Fellingham, I think, would like to go to bed, papa," said Annette.

"Miss Smith must be getting cold," Fellingham hinted.

"Bounce away indoors," replied Van Diemen, and he led them like a bull.

Annette was disinclined to leave them together in the smoking-room, and under the pretext of wishing to see her father to bed she remained with them, though there was a novel directness and heat of tone in Herbert that alarmed her, and with reason. He divined in hideous outlines what had happened. He was no longer figuring on easy ice, but desperate at the prospect of a loss to himself, and a fate for Annette, that tossed him from repulsion to incredulity, and so back.

Van Diemen begged him to light his pipe.

"I'm off to London to-morrow," said Fellingham. "I don't want to go, for very particular reasons; I may be of more use there. I have a cousin who's a General officer in the army, and if I have your permission—you see, anything's better, as it seems to me, than that you should depend for peace and comfort on one man's tongue not wagging, especially when he is not the best of tempers if I have your permission—without mentioning names, of course—I'll consult him."

There was a dead silence.

"You know you may trust me, sir. I love your daughter with all my heart.
Your honour and your interests are mine."

Van Diemen struggled for composure.

"Netty, what have you been at?" he said.

"It is untrue, papa!" she answered the unworded accusation.

"Annette has told me nothing, sir. I have heard it. You must brace your mind to the fact that it is known. What is known to Mr. Tinman is pretty sure to be known generally at the next disagreement."

"That scoundrel Mart!" Van Diemen muttered.

"I am positive Mr. Tinman did not speak of you, papa," said Annette, and turned her eyes from the half-paralyzed figure of her father on Herbert to put him to proof.

"No, but he made himself heard when it was being discussed. At any rate, it's known; and the thing to do is to meet it."

"I'm off. I'll not stop a day. I'd rather live on the Continent," said Van Diemen, shaking himself, as to prepare for the step into that desert.

"Mr. Tinman has been most generous!" Annette protested tearfully.

"I won't say no: I think you are deceived and lend him your own generosity," said Herbert. "Can you suppose it generous, that even in the extremest case, he should speak of the matter to your father, and talk of denouncing him? He did it."

"He was provoked."

"A gentleman is distinguished by his not allowing himself to be provoked."

"I am engaged to him, and I cannot hear it said that he is not a gentleman."

The first part of her sentence Annette uttered bravely; at the conclusion she broke down. She wished Herbert to be aware of the truth, that he might stay his attacks on Mr. Tinman; and she believed he had only been guessing the circumstances in which her father was placed; but the comparison between her two suitors forced itself on her now, when the younger one spoke in a manner so self-contained, brief, and full of feeling.

She had to leave the room weeping.

"Has your daughter engaged herself, sir?" said Herbert,

"Talk to me to-morrow; don't give us up if she has we were trapped, it's my opinion," said Van Diemen. "There's the devil in that wine of — Mart Tinman's. I feel it still, and in the morning it'll be worse. What can she see in him? I must quit the country; carry her off. How he did it, I don't know. It was that woman, the widow, the fellow's sister. She talked till she piped her eye — talked about our lasting union. On my soul, I believe I egged Netty on! I was in a mollified way with that wine; all of a sudden the woman joins their hands! And I — a man of spirit will despise me! — what I thought of was, "now my secret's safe! You've sobered me, young sir. I see myself, if that's being sober. I don't ask your opinion of me; I am a deserter, false to my colours, a breaker of his oath. Only mark this: I was married, and a common trooper, married to a handsome young woman, true as steel; but she was handsome, and we were starvation poor, and she had to endure persecution from an officer day by day. Bear that situation in your mind. . . . Providence dropped me a hundred pounds out of the sky. Properly speaking, it popped up out of the earth, for I reaped it, you may say, from a relative's grave. Rich and poor 's all right, if I'm rich and you're poor; and you may be happy though you're poor; but where there are many poor young women, lots of rich men are a terrible temptation to them. That's my dear good wife speaking, and had she been spared to me I never should have come back to Old England, and heart's delight and heartache I should not have known. She was my backbone, she was my breast-comforter too. Why did she stick to me? Because I had faith in her when appearances were against her. But she never forgave this country the hurt to her woman's pride. You'll have noticed a squarish jaw in Netty. That's her mother. And I shall have to encounter it, supposing I find Mart Tinman has been playing me false. I'm blown on somehow. I'll think of what course I'll take 'twixt now and morning. Good night, young gentleman."

"Good night; sir," said Herbert, adding, "I will get information from the Horse Guards; as for the people knowing it about here, you're not living much in society — "

"It's not other people's feelings, it's my own," Van Diemen silenced him. "I feel it, if it's in the wind; ever since Mart Tinman spoke the thing out, I've felt on my skin cold and hot."

He flourished his lighted candle and went to bed, manifestly solaced by the idea that he was the victim of his own feelings.

Herbert could not sleep. Annette's monstrous choice of Tinman in preference to himself constantly assailed and shook his understanding. There was the "squarish jaw" mentioned by her father to think of. It filled him with a vague apprehension, but he was unable to imagine that a young girl, and an English girl, and an enthusiastic young English girl, could be devoid of sentiment; and presuming her to have it, as one must, there was no fear, that she would persist in her loathsome choice when she knew her father was against it.

CHAPTER IX

Annette did not shun him next morning. She did not shun the subject, either. But she had been exact in arranging that she should not be more than a few minutes downstairs before her father. Herbert found, that compared with her, girls of sentiment are commonplace indeed. She had conceived an insane idea of nobility in Tinman that blinded her to his face, figure, and character — his manners, likewise. He had forgiven a blow!

Silly as the delusion might be, it clothed her in whimsical attractiveness.

It was a beauty in her to dwell so firmly upon moral quality. Overthrown and stunned as he was, and reduced to helplessness by her brief and positive replies, Herbert was obliged to admire the singular young lady, who spoke, without much shyness, of her incongruous, destined mate though his admiration had an edge cutting like irony. While in the turn for candour, she ought to have told him, that previous to her decision she had weighed the case of the diverse claims of himself and Tinman, and resolved them according to her predilection for the peaceful residence of her father and herself in England. This she had done a little regretfully, because of the natural sympathy of the young girl for the younger man. But the younger man had seemed to her seriously- straightforward mind too light and airy in his wooing, like one of her waltzing officers — very well so long as she stepped the measure with him, and not forcible enough to take her off her feet. He had changed, and now that he had become persuasive, she feared he would disturb the serenity with which she desired and strove to contemplate her decision. Tinman's magnanimity was present in her imagination to sustain her, though she was aware that Mrs. Cavely had surprised her will, and caused it to surrender unconsulted by her wiser intelligence.

"I cannot listen to you," she said to Herbert, after listening longer than was prudent. "If what you say of papa is true, I do not think he will remain in Crikswich, or even in England. But I am sure the old friend we used, to speak of so much in Australia has not wilfully betrayed him."

Herbert would have had to say, "Look on us two!" to proceed in his baffled wooing; and the very ludicrousness of the contrast led him to see the folly and shame of proposing it.

Van Diemen came down to breakfast looking haggard and restless. "I have 'nt had my morning's walk—I can't go out to be hooted," he said, calling to his daughter for tea, and strong tea; and explaining to Herbert that he knew it to be bad for the nerves, but it was an antidote to bad champagne.

Mr. Herbert Fellingham had previously received an invitation on behalf of a sister of his to Crikswich. A dull sense of genuine sagacity inspired him to remind Annette of it. She wrote prettily to Miss Mary Fellingham, and Herbert had some faint joy in carrying away the letter of her handwriting.

"Fetch her soon, for we sha'n't be here long," Van Diemen said to him at parting. He expressed a certain dread of his next meeting with Mart Tinman.

Herbert speedily brought Mary Fellingham to Elba, and left her there. The situation was apparently unaltered. Van Diemen looked worn, like a man who has been feeding mainly on his reflections, which was manifest in his few melancholy bits of speech. He said to Herbert: "How you feel a thing when you are found out!" and, "It doesn't do for a man with a heart to do wrong!" He designated the two principal roads by which poor sinners come to a conscience. His own would have slumbered but for discovery; and, as he remarked, if it had not been for his heart leading him to Tinman, he would not have fallen into that man's power.

The arrival of a young lady of fashionable appearance at Elba was matter of cogitation to Mrs. Cavely. She was disposed to suspect that it meant something, and Van Diemen's behaviour to her brother would of itself have fortified any suspicion. He did not call at the house on the beach, he did not invite Martin to dinner, he was rarely seen, and when he appeared at the Town Council he once or twice violently opposed his friend Martin, who came home ruffled, deeply offended in his interests and his dignity.

"Have you noticed any difference in Annette's treatment of you, dear?"
Mrs. Cavely inquired.

"No," said Tinman; "none. She shakes hands. She asks after my health. She offers me my cup of tea."

"I have seen all that. But does she avoid privacy with you?"

"Dear me, no! Why should she? I hope, Martha, I am a man who may be confided in by any young lady in England."

"I am sure you may, dear Martin."

"She has an objection to name the . . . the day," said Martin. "I have informed her that I have an objection to long engagements. I don't like her new companion: She says she has been presented at Court. I greatly doubt it."

"It's to give herself a style, you may depend. I don't believe her!" exclaimed Mrs. Cavely, with sharp personal asperity.

Brother and sister examined together the Court Guide they had purchased on the occasion at once of their largest outlay and most thrilling gratification; in it they certainly found the name of General Fellingham. "But he can't be related to a newspaper-writer," said Mrs. Cavely.

To which her brother rejoined, "Unless the young man turned scamp. I hate unproductive professions."

"I hate him, Martin." Mrs. Cavely laughed in scorn, "I should say, I pity him. It's as clear to me as the sun at noonday, he wanted Annette. That's why I was in a hurry. How I dreaded he would come that evening to our dinner! When I saw him absent, I could have cried out it was Providence! And so be careful—we have had everything done for us from on High as yet—but be careful of your temper, dear Martin. I will hasten on the union; for it's a shame of a girl to drag a man behind her till he's old at the altar. Temper, dear, if you will only think of it, is the weak point."

"Now he has begun boasting to me of his Australian wines!" Tinman ejaculated.

"Bear it. Bear it as you do Gippsland. My dear, you have the retort in your heart: — Yes! but have you a Court in Australia?"

"Ha! and his Australian wines cost twice the amount I pay for mine!"

"Quite true. We are not obliged to buy them, I should hope. I would, though — a dozen — if I thought it necessary, to keep him quiet."

Tinman continued muttering angrily over the Australian wines, with a word of irritation at Gippsland, while promising to be watchful of his temper.

"What good is Australia to us," he asked, "if it does n't bring us money?"

"It's going to, my dear," said Mrs. Cavely. "Think of that when he begins boasting his Australia. And though it's convict's money, as he confesses — "

"With his convict's money!" Tinman interjected tremblingly. "How long am I expected to wait?"

"Rely on me to hurry on the day," said Mrs. Cavely. "There is no other annoyance?"

"Wherever I am going to buy, that man outbids me and then says it's the old country's want of pluck and dash, and doing things large-handed! A man who'd go on his knees to stop in England!" Tinman vociferated in a breath; and fairly reddened by the effort: "He may have to do it yet. I can't stand insult."

"You are less able to stand insult after Honours," his sister said, in obedience to what she had observed of him since his famous visit to London. "It must be so, in nature. But temper is everything just now. Remember, it was by command of temper, and letting her father put himself in the wrong, you got hold of Annette. And I would abstain even from wine. For sometimes after it, you have owned it disagreed. And I have noticed these eruptions between you and Mr. Smith — as he calls himself — generally after wine."

"Always the poor! the poor! money for the poor!" Tinman harped on further grievances against Van Diemen. "I say doctors have said the drain on the common is healthy; it's a healthy smell, nourishing. We've always had it and been a healthy town. But the sea encroaches, and I say my house and my property is in danger. He buys my house over my head, and offers me the Crouch to live in at an advanced rent. And then he sells me my house at an advanced price, and I buy, and then he votes against a penny for the protection of the shore! And we're in Winter again! As if he was not in my power!"

"My dear Martin, to Elba we go, and soon, if you will govern your temper," said Mrs. Cavely. "You're an angel to let me speak of it so, and it's only that man that irritates you. I call him sinfully ostentatious."

"I could blow him from a gun if I spoke out, and he knows it! He's wanting in common gratitude, let alone respect," Tinman snorted.

"But he has a daughter, my dear."

Tinman slowly and crackingly subsided.

His main grievance against Van Diemen was the non-recognition of his importance by that uncultured Australian, who did not seem to be conscious of the dignities and distinctions we come to in our country. The moneyed daughter, the prospective marriage, for an economical man rejected by every lady surrounding him, advised him to lock up his temper in submission to Martha.

"Bring Annette to dine with us," he said, on Martha's proposing a visit to the dear young creature.

Martha drank a glass of her brother's wine at lunch, and departed on the mission.

Annette declined to be brought. Her excuse was her guest, Miss Fellingham.

"Bring her too, by all means — if you'll condescend, I am sure," Mrs. Cavely said to Mary.

"I am much obliged to you; I do not dine out at present," said the London lady.

"Dear me! are you ill?"

"No."

"Nothing in the family, I hope?"

"My family?"

"I am sure, I beg pardon," said Mrs. Cavely, bridling with a spite pardonable by the severest moralist.

"Can I speak to you alone?" she addressed Annette.

Miss Fellingham rose.

Mrs. Cavely confronted her. "I can't allow it; I can't think of it. I'm only taking a little liberty with one I may call my future sister-in-law."

"Shall I come out with you?" said Annette, in sheer lassitude assisting Mary Fellingham in her scheme to show the distastefulness of this lady and her brother.

"Not if you don't wish to."

"I have no objection."

"Another time will do."

"Will you write?"

"By post indeed!"

Mrs. Cavely delivered a laugh supposed to, be peculiar to the English stage.

"It would be a penny thrown away," said Annette. "I thought you could send a messenger."

Intercommunication with Miss Fellingham had done mischief to her high moral conception of the pair inhabiting the house on the beach. Mrs. Cavely saw it, and could not conceal that she smarted.

Her counsel to her brother, after recounting the offensive scene to him in animated dialogue, was, to give Van Diemen a fright.

"I wish I had not drunk that glass of sherry before starting," she exclaimed, both savagely and sagcly. "It's best after business. And these gentlemen's habits of yours of taking to dining late upset me. I'm afraid I showed temper; but you, Martin, would not have borne one- tenth of what I did."

"How dare you say so!" her brother rebuked her indignantly; and the house on the beach enclosed with difficulty a storm between brother and sister, happily not heard outside, because of loud winds raging.

Nevertheless Tinman pondered on Martha's idea of the wisdom of giving Van
Diemen a fright.

CHAPTER X

The English have been called a bad-tempered people, but this is to judge of them by their manifestations; whereas an examination into causes might prove them to be no worse tempered than that man is a bad sleeper who lies in a biting bed. If a sagacious instinct directs them to discountenance realistic tales, the realistic tale should justify its appearance by the discovery of an apology for the tormented souls. Once they sang madrigals, once they danced on the green, they revelled in their lusty humours, without having recourse to the pun for fun, an exhibition of hundreds of bare legs for jollity, a sentimental wailing all in the throat for music. Evidence is procurable that they have been an artificially-reared people, feeding on the genius of inventors, transposers, adulterators, instead of the products of nature, for the last half century; and it is unfair to affirm of them that they are positively this or that. They are experiments. They are the sons and victims of a desperate Energy, alluring by cheapness, satiating with quantity, that it may mount in the social scale, at the expense of their tissues. The land is in a state of fermentation to mount, and the shop, which has shot half their stars to their social zenith, is what verily they would scald themselves to wash themselves free of. Nor is it in any degree a reprehensible sign that they should fly as from hue and cry the title of tradesman. It is on the contrary the spot of sanity, which bids us right cordially hope. Energy, transferred to the moral sense, may clear them yet.

Meanwhile this beer, this wine, both are of a character to have killed more than the tempers of a less gifted people. Martin Tinman invited Van Diemen Smith to try the flavour of a wine that, as he said, he thought of "laying down."

It has been hinted before of a strange effect upon the minds of men who knew what they were going to, when they received an invitation to dine with Tinman. For the sake of a little social meeting at any cost, they accepted it; accepted it with a sigh, midway as by engineering measurement between prospective and retrospective; as nearly mechanical as things human may be, like the Mussulman's accustomed cry of Kismet. Has it not been related of the little Jew babe sucking at its mother's breast in Jerusalem, that this innocent, long after the Captivity, would start convulsively, relinquishing its feast, and indulging in the purest. Hebrew lamentation of the most tenacious of races, at the passing sound of a Babylonian or a Ninevite voice? In some such manner did men, unable to refuse, deep in what remained to them of nature, listen to Tinman; and so did Van Diemen, sighing heavily under the operation of simple animal instinct.

"You seem miserable," said Tinman, not oblivious of his design to give his friend a fright.

"Do I? No, I'm all right," Van Diemen replied. "I'm thinking of alterations at the Hall before Summer, to accommodate guests—if I stay here."

"I suppose you would not like to be separated from Annette."

"Separated? No, I should think I shouldn't. Who'd do it?"

"Because I should not like to leave my good sister Martha all to herself in a house so near the sea—"

"Why not go to the Crouch, man?"

"Thank you."

"No thanks needed if you don't take advantage of the offer."

They were at the entrance to Elba, whither Mr. Tinman was betaking himself to see his intended. He asked if Annette was at home, and to his great stupefaction heard that she had gone to London for a week.

Dissembling the spite aroused within him, he postponed his very strongly fortified design, and said, "You must be lonely."

Van Diemen informed him that it would be for a night only, as young Fellingham was coming down to keep him company.

"At six o'clock this evening, then," said Tinman. "We're not fashionable in Winter."

"Hang me, if I know when ever we were!" Van Diemen rejoined.

"Come, though, you'd like to be. You've got your ambition, Philip, like other men."

"Respectable and respected—that's my ambition, Mr. Mart."

Tinman simpered: "With your wealth!"

"Ay, I'm rich—for a contented mind."

"I'm pretty sure you'll approve my new vintage," said Tinman. "It's direct from Oporto, my wine-merchant tells me, on his word."

"What's the price?"

"No, no, no. Try it first. It's rather a stiff price."

Van Diemen was partially reassured by the announcement. "What do you call a stiff price?"

"Well!—over thirty."

"Double that, and you may have a chance."

"Now," cried Tinman, exasperated, "how can a man from Australia know anything about prices for port? You can't divest your ideas of diggers' prices. You're like an intoxicating drink yourself on the tradesmen of our town. You think it fine—ha! ha! I daresay, Philip, I should be doing the same if I were up to your mark at my banker's. We can't all of us be lords, nor baronets."

Catching up his temper thus cleverly, he curbed that habitual runaway, and retired from his old friend's presence to explode in the society of the solitary Martha.

Annette's behaviour was as bitterly criticized by the sister as by the brother.

"She has gone to those Fellingham people; and she may be thinking of jilting us," Mrs. Cavely said.

"In that case, I have no mercy," cried her brother. "I have borne"—he bowed with a professional spiritual humility—"as I should, but it may get past endurance. I say I have borne enough; and if the worst comes to the worst, and I hand him over to the authorities—I say I mean him no harm, but he has struck me. He beat me as a boy and he has struck me as a man, and I say I have no thought of revenge, but I cannot have him here; and I say if I drive him out of the country back to his Gippsland!"

Martin Tinman quivered for speech, probably for that which feedeth speech, as is the way with angry men.

"And what?—what then?" said Martha, with the tender mellifluousness of sisterly reproach. "What good can you expect of letting temper get the better of you, dear?"

Tinman did not enjoy her recent turn for usurping the lead in their consultations, and he said, tartly, "This good, Martha. We shall get the Hall at my price, and be Head People here. Which," he raised his note, "which he, a Deserter, has no right to pretend to give himself out to be. What your feelings may be as an old inhabitant, I don't know, but I have always looked up to the people at Elba Hall, and I say I don't like to have a Deserter squandering convict's money there—with his forty-pound- a-year cook, and his champagne at seventy a dozen. It's the luxury of Sodom and Gomorrah."

"That does not prevent its being very nice to dine there," said Mrs. Cavely; "and it shall be our table for good if I have any management."

"You mean me, ma'am," bellowed Tinman.

"Not at all," she breathed, in dulcet contrast. "You are good-looking, Martin, but you have not half such pretty eyes as the person I mean. I never ventured to dream of managing you, Martin. I am thinking of the people at Elba."

"But why this extraordinary treatment of me, Martha?"

"She's a child, having her head turned by those Fellinghams. But she's honourable; she has sworn to me she would be honourable."

"You do think I may as well give him a fright?" Tinman inquired hungrily.

"A sort of hint; but very gentle, Martin. Do be gentle—casual like—as if you did n't want to say it. Get him on his Gippsland. Then if he brings you to words, you can always laugh back, and say you will go to Kew and see the Fernery, and fancy all that, so high, on Helvellyn or the Downs. Why"—Mrs. Cavely, at the end of her astute advices and cautionings, as usual, gave loose to her natural character — "Why that man came back to England at all, with his boastings of Gippsland, I can't for the life of me find out. It's a perfect mystery."

"It is," Tinman sounded his voice at a great depth, reflectively. Glad of taking the part she was perpetually assuming of late, he put out his hand and said: "But it may have been ordained for our good, Martha."

"True, dear," said she, with an earnest sentiment of thankfulness to the
Power which had led him round to her way of thinking and feeling.

CHAPTER XI

Annette had gone to the big metropolis, which burns in colonial imaginations as the sun of cities, and was about to see something of London, under the excellent auspices of her new friend, Mary Fellingham, and a dense fog. She was alarmed by the darkness, a little in fear, too, of Herbert; and these feelings caused her to chide herself for leaving her father.

Hearing her speak of her father sadly, Herbert kindly proposed to go down to Crikswich on the very day of her coming. She thanked him, and gave him a taste of bitterness by smiling favourably on his offer; but as he wished her to discern and take to heart the difference between one man and another, in the light of a suitor, he let her perceive that it cost him heavy pangs to depart immediately, and left her to brood on his example. Mary Fellingham liked Annette. She thought her a sensible girl of uncultivated sensibilities, the reverse of thousands; not commonplace, therefore; and that the sensibilities were expanding was to be seen in her gradual unreadiness to talk of her engagement to Mr. Tinman, though her intimacy with Mary warmed daily. She considered she was bound to marry the man at some distant date, and did not feel unhappiness yet. She had only felt uneasy when she had to greet and converse with her intended; especially when the London young lady had been present. Herbert's departure relieved her of the pressing sense of contrast. She praised him to Mary for his extreme kindness to her father, and down in her unsounded heart desired that her father might appreciate it even more than she did.

Herbert drove into Crikswich at night, and stopped at Crickledon's, where he heard that Van Diemen was dining with Tinman.

Crickledon the carpenter permitted certain dry curves to play round his lips like miniature shavings at the name of Tinman; but Herbert asked, "What is it now?" in vain, and he went to Crickledon the cook.

This union of the two Crickledons, male and female; was an ideal one, such as poor women dream of; and men would do the same, if they knew how poor they are. Each had a profession, each was independent of the other, each supported the fabric. Consequently there was mutual respect, as between two pillars of a house. Each saw the other's faults with a sly wink to the world, and an occasional interchange of sarcasm that was tonic, very strengthening to the wits without endangering the habit of affection. Crickledon the cook stood for her own opinions, and directed the public conduct of Crickledon the carpenter; and if he went astray from the line she marked out, she put it down to human nature, to which she was tolerant. He, when she had not followed his advice, ascribed it to the nature of women. She never said she was the equal of her husband; but the carpenter proudly acknowledged that she was as good as a man, and he bore with foibles derogatory to such high stature, by teaching himself to observe a neatness of domestic and general management that told him he certainly was not as good as a woman. Herbert delighted in them. The cook regaled the carpenter with skilful, tasty, and economic dishes; and the carpenter, obedient to her supplications, had promised, in the event of his outliving her, that no hands but his should have the making of her coffin. "It is so nice," she said, "to think one's own husband will put together the box you are to lie in, of his own make!" Had they been even a doubtfully united pair, the cook's anticipation of a comfortable coffin, the work of the best carpenter in England, would have kept them together; and that which fine cookery does for the cementing of couples needs not to be recounted to those who have read a chapter or two of the natural history of the male sex.

"Crickledon, my dear soul, your husband is labouring with a bit of fun,"
Herbert said to her.

"He would n't laugh loud at Punch, for fear of an action," she replied. "He never laughs out till he gets to bed, and has locked the door; and when he does he says 'Hush!' to me. Tinman is n't bailiff again just yet, and where he has his bailiff's best Court suit from, you may ask. He exercises in it off and on all the week, at night, and sometimes in the middle of the day."

Herbert rallied her for her gossip's credulity.

"It's truth," she declared. "I have it from the maid of the house, little Jane, whom he pays four pound a year for all the work of the house: a clever little thing with her hands and her head she is; and can read and write beautiful; and she's a mind to leave 'em if they don't advance her. She knocked and went in while he was full blaze, and bowing his poll to his glass. And now he turns the key, and a child might know he was at it."

"He can't be such a donkey!"

"And he's been seen at the window on the seaside. 'Who's your Admiral staying at the house on the beach?' men have inquired as they come ashore. My husband has heard it. Tinman's got it on his brain. He might be cured by marriage to a sound-headed woman, but he 'll soon be wanting to walk about in silk legs if he stops a bachelor. They tell me his old mother here had a dress value twenty pound; and pomp's inherited. Save as he may, there's his leak."

Herbert's contempt for Tinman was intense; it was that of the young and ignorant who live in their imaginations like spendthrifts, unaware of the importance of them as the food of life, and of how necessary it is to seize upon the solider one among them for perpetual sustenance when the unsubstantial are vanishing. The great event of his bailiff's term of office had become the sun of Tinman's system. He basked in its rays. He meant to be again the proud official, royally distinguished; meantime, though he knew not that his days were dull, he groaned under the dulness; and, as cart or cab horses, uncomplaining as a rule, show their view of the nature of harness when they have release to frisk in a field, it is possible that existence was made tolerable to the jogging man by some minutes of excitement in his bailiff's Court suit. Really to pasture on our recollections we ought to dramatize them. There is, however, only the testimony of a maid and a mariner to show that Tinman did it, and those are witnesses coming of particularly long-bow classes, given to magnify small items of fact.

On reaching the hall Herbert found the fire alight in the smoking-room, and soon after settling himself there he heard Van Diemen's voice at the hall-door saying good night to Tinman.

"Thank the Lord! there you are," said Van Diemen, entering the room. "I couldn't have hoped so much. That rascal!" he turned round to the door. "He has been threatening me, and then smoothing me. Hang his oil! It's combustible. And hang the port he's for laying down, as he calls it. 'Leave it to posterity,' says I. 'Why?' says he. 'Because the young ones 'll be better able to take care of themselves,' says I, and he insists on an explanation. I gave it to him. Out he bursts like a wasp's nest. He may have said what he did say in temper. He seemed sorry afterwards—poor old Mart! The scoundrel talked of Horse Guards and telegraph wires."

"Scoundrel, but more ninny," said Herbert, full of his contempt. "Dare him to do his worst. The General tells me they 'd be glad to overlook it at the Guards, even if they had all the facts. Branding 's out of the question."

"I swear it was done in my time," cried Van Diemen, all on fire.

"It's out of the question. You might be advised to leave England for a few months. As for the society here—"

"If I leave, I leave for good. My heart's broken. I'm disappointed. I'm deceived in my friend. He and I in the old days! What's come to him? What on earth is it changes men who stop in England so? It can't be the climate. And did you mention my name to General Fellingham?"

"Certainly not," said Herbert. "But listen to me, sir, a moment. Why not get together half-a-dozen friends of the neighbourhood, and make a clean breast of it. Englishmen like that kind of manliness, and they are sure to ring sound to it."

"I couldn't!" Van Diemen sighed. "It's not a natural feeling I have about it—I 've brooded on the word. If I have a nightmare, I see Deserter written in sulphur on the black wall."

"You can't remain at his mercy, and be bullied as you are. He makes you ill, sir. He won't do anything, but he'll go on worrying you. I'd stop him at once. I'd take the train to-morrow and get an introduction to the Commander-in-Chief. He's the very man to be kind to you in a situation like this. The General would get you the introduction."

"That's more to my taste; but no, I couldn't," Van Diemen moaned in his weakness. "Money has unmanned me. I was n't this kind of man formerly; nor more was Mart Tinman, the traitor! All the world seems changeing for the worse, and England is n't what she used to be."

"You let that man spoil it for you, sir." Herbert related Mrs. Crickledon's tale of Mr. Tinman, adding, "He's an utter donkey. I should defy him. What I should do would be to let him know to-morrow morning that you don't intend to see him again. Blow for, blow, is the thing he requires. He'll be cringing to you in a week."

"And you'd like to marry Annette," said Van Diemen, relishing, nevertheless, the advice, whose origin and object he perceived so plainly.

"Of course I should," said Herbert, franker still in his colour than his speech.

"I don't see him my girl's husband." Van Diemen eyed the red hollow in the falling coals. "When I came first, and found him a healthy man, good-looking enough for a trifle over forty, I 'd have given her gladly, she nodding Yes. Now all my fear is she's in earnest. Upon my soul, I had the notion old Mart was a sort of a boy still; playing man, you know. But how can you understand? I fancied his airs and stiffness were put on; thought I saw him burning true behind it. Who can tell? He seems to be jealous of my buying property in his native town. Something frets him. I ought never to have struck him! There's my error, and I repent it. Strike a friend! I wonder he didn't go off to the Horse Guards at once. I might have done it in his place, if I found I couldn't lick him. I should have tried kicking first."

"Yes, shinning before peaching," said Herbert, astonished almost as much as he was disgusted by the inveterate sentimental attachment of Van Diemen to his old friend.

Martin Tinman anticipated good things of the fright he had given the man after dinner. He had, undoubtedly, yielded to temper, forgetting pure policy, which it is so exceeding difficult to practice. But he had soothed the startled beast; they had shaken hands at parting, and Tinman hoped that the week of Annette's absence would enable him to mould her father. Young Fellingham's appointment to come to Elba had slipped Mr. Tinman's memory. It was annoying to see this intruder. "At all events, he's not with Annette," said Mrs. Cavely. "How long has her father to run on?"

"Five months," Tinman replied. "He would have completed his term of service in five months."

"And to think of his being a rich man because he deserted," Mrs. Cavely interjected. "Oh! I do call it immoral. He ought to be apprehended and punished, to be an example for the good of society. If you lose time, my dear Martin, your chance is gone. He's wriggling now. And if I could believe he talked us over to that young impudent, who has n't a penny that he does n't get from his pen, I'd say, denounce him to-morrow. I long for Elba. I hate this house. It will be swallowed up some day; I know it; I have dreamt it. Elba at any cost. Depend upon it, Martin, you have been foiled in your suits on account of the mean house you inhabit. Enter Elba as that girl's husband, or go there to own it, and girls will crawl to you."

"You are a ridiculous woman, Martha," said Tinman, not dissenting.

The mixture of an idea of public duty with a feeling of personal rancour is a strong incentive to the pursuit of a stern line of conduct; and the glimmer of self-interest superadded does not check the steps of the moralist. Nevertheless, Tinman held himself in. He loved peace. He preached it, he disseminated it. At a meeting in the town he strove to win Van Diemen's voice in favour of a vote for further moneys to protect 'our shores.'" Van Diemen laughed at him, telling him he wanted a battery. "No," said Tinman, "I've had enough to do with soldiers."

"How's that?"

"They might be more cautious. I say, they might learn to know their friends from their enemies."

"That's it, that's it," said Van Diemen. "If you say much more, my hearty, you'll find me bidding against you next week for Marine Parade and Belle Vue Terrace. I've a cute eye for property, and this town's looking up."

"You look about you before you speculate in land and house property here," retorted Tinman.

Van Diemen bore so much from him that he asked himself whether he could be an Englishman. The title of Deserter was his raw wound. He attempted to form the habit of stigmatizing himself with it in the privacy of his chamber, and he succeeded in establishing the habit of talking to himself, so that he was heard by the household, and Annette, on her return, was obliged to warn him of his indiscretion. This development of a new weakness exasperated him. Rather to prove his courage by defiance than to baffle Tinman's ambition to become the principal owner of houses in Crikswich, by outbidding him at the auction for the sale of Marine Parade and Belle Vue Terrace, Van Diemen ran the houses up at the auction, and ultimately had Belle Vue knocked down to him. So fierce was the quarrel that Annette, in conjunction with Mrs. Cavely; was called on to interpose with her sweetest grace. "My native place," Tinman said to her; "it is my native place. I have a pride in it; I desire to own property in it, and your father opposes me. He opposes me. Then says I may have it back at auction price, after he has gone far to double the price! I have borne—I repeat I have borne too much."

"Are n't your properties to be equal to one?" said Mrs. Cavely, smiling mother—like from Tinman to Annette.

He sought to produce a fondling eye in a wry face, and said, "Yes, I will remember that."

"Annette will bless you with her dear hand in a month or two at the outside," Mrs. Cavely murmured, cherishingly.

"She will?" Tinman cracked his body to bend to her.

"Oh, I cannot say; do not distress me. Be friendly with papa," the girl resumed, moving to escape.

"That is the essential," said Mrs. Cavely; and continued, when Annette had gone, "The essential is to get over the next few months, miss, and then to snap your fingers at us. Martin, I would force that man to sell you Belle Vue under the price he paid for it, just to try your power."

Tinman was not quite so forcible. He obtained Belle Vue at auction price, and his passion for revenge was tipped with fire by having it accorded as a friend's favour.

The poisoned state of his mind was increased by a December high wind that rattled his casements, and warned him of his accession of property exposed to the elements. Both he and his sister attributed their nervousness to the sinister behaviour of Van Diemen. For the house on the beach had only, in most distant times, been threatened by the sea, and no house on earth was better protected from man,—

Neptune, in the shape of a coastguard, being paid by Government to patrol about it during the hours of darkness. They had never had any fears before Van Diemen arrived, and caused them to give thrice their ordinary number of dinners to guests per annum. In fact, before Van Diemen came, the house on the beach looked on Crikswich without a rival to challenge its anticipated lordship over the place, and for some inexplicable reason it seemed to its inhabitants to have been a safer as well as a happier residence.

They were consoled by Tinman's performance of a clever stroke in privately purchasing the cottages west of the town, and including Crickledon's shop, abutting on Marine Parade. Then from the house on the beach they looked at an entire frontage of their property.

They entered the month of February. No further time was to be lost, "or we shall wake up to find that man has fooled us," Mrs. Cavely said. Tinman appeared at Elba to demand a private interview with Annette. His hat was blown into the hall as the door opened to him, and he himself was glad to be sheltered by the door, so violent was the gale. Annette and her father were sitting together. They kept the betrothed gentleman waiting a very long time. At last Van Diemen went to him, and said, "Netty 'll see you, if you must. I suppose you have no business with me?"

"Not to-day," Tinman replied.

Van Diemen strode round the drawing-room with his hands in his pockets. "There's a disparity of ages," he said, abruptly, as if desirous to pour out his lesson while he remembered it. "A man upwards of forty marries a girl under twenty, he's over sixty before she's forty; he's decaying when she's only mellow. I ought never to have struck you, I know. And you're such an infernal bad temper at times, and age does n't improve that, they say; and she's been educated tip-top. She's sharp on grammar, and a man may n't like that much when he's a husband. See her, if you must. But she does n't take to the idea; there's the truth. Disparity of ages and unsuitableness of dispositions — what was it Fellingham said? — like two barrel-organs grinding different tunes all day in a house."

"I don't want to hear Mr. Fellingham's comparisons," Tinman snapped.

"Oh! he's nothing to the girl," said Van Diemen. "She doesn't stomach leaving me."

"My dear Philip! why should she leave you? When we have interests in common as one household —"

"She says you're such a damned bad temper."

Tinman was pursuing amicably, "When we are united —" But the frightful charge brought against his temper drew him up. "Fiery I may be. Annette has seen I am forgiving. I am a Christian. You have provoked me; you have struck me."

"I 'll give you a couple of thousand pounds in hard money to be off the bargain, and not bother the girl," said Van Diemen.

"Now," rejoined Tinman, "I am offended. I like money, like most men who have made it. You do, Philip. But I don't come courting like a pauper. Not for ten thousand; not for twenty. Money cannot be a compensation to me for the loss of Annette. I say I love Annette."

"Because," Van Diemen continued his speech, "you trapped us into that engagement, Mart. You dosed me with the stuff you buy for wine, while your sister sat sugaring and mollifying my girl; and she did the trick in a minute, taking Netty by surprise when I was all heart and no head; and since that you may have seen the girl turn her head from marriage like my woods from the wind."

"Mr. Van Diemen Smith!" Tinman panted; he mastered himself. "You shall not provoke me. My introductions of you in this neighbourhood, my patronage, prove my friendship."

"You'll be a good old fellow, Mart, when you get over your hopes of being knighted."

"Mr. Fellingham may set you against my wine, Philip. Let me tell you — I know you — you would not object to have your daughter called Lady."

"With a spindle-shanked husband capering in a Court suit before he goes to bed every night, that he may n't forget what a fine fellow he was one day bygone! You're growing lean on it, Mart, like a recollection fifty years old."

"You have never forgiven me that day, Philip!"

"Jealous, am I? Take the money, give up the girl, and see what friends we'll be. I'll back your buyings, I'll advertise your sellings. I'll pay a painter to paint you in your Court suit, and hang up a copy of you in my diningroom."

"Annette is here," said Tinman, who had been showing Etna's tokens of insurgency.

He admired Annette. Not till latterly had Herbert Fellingham been so true an admirer of Annette as Tinman was. She looked sincere and she dressed inexpensively. For these reasons she was the best example of womankind that he knew, and her enthusiasm for England had the sympathetic effect on him of obscuring the rest of the world, and thrilling him with the reassuring belief that he was blest in his blood and his birthplace—points which her father, with his boastings of Gippsland, and other people talking of scenes on the Continent, sometimes disturbed in his mind.

"Annette," said he, "I come requesting to converse with you in private."

"If you wish it—I would rather not," she answered.

Tinman raised his head, as often at Helmstone when some offending shopwoman was to hear her doom.

He bent to her. "I see. Before your father, then!"

"It isn't an agreeable bit of business, to me," Van Diemen grumbled, frowning and shrugging.

"I have come, Annette, to ask you, to beg you, entreat—before a third person—laughing, Philip?"

"The wrong side of my mouth, my friend. And I'll tell you what: we're in for heavy seas, and I 'm not sorry you've taken the house on the beach off my hands."

"Pray, Mr. Tinman, speak at once, if you please, and I will do my best. Papa vexes you."

"No, no," replied Tinman.

He renewed his commencement. Van Diemen interrupted him again.

"Hang your power over me, as you call it. Eh, old Mart? I'm a Deserter. I'll pay a thousand pounds to the British army, whether they punish me or not. March me off tomorrow!"

"Papa, you are unjust, unkind." Annette turned to him in tears.

"No, no," said Tinman, "I do not feel it. Your father has misunderstood me, Annette."

"I am sure he has," she said fervently. "And, Mr. Tinman, I will faithfully promise that so long as you are good to my dear father, I will not be untrue to my engagement, only do not wish me to name any day. We shall be such very good dear friends if you consent to this. Will you?"

Pausing for a space, the enamoured man unrolled his voice in lamentation:
"Oh! Annette, how long will you keep me?"

"There; you'll set her crying!" said Van Diemen. "Now you can run upstairs, Netty. By jingo! Mart Tinman, you've got a bass voice for love affairs."

"Annette," Tinman called to her, and made her turn round as she was retiring. "I must know the day before the end of winter. Please. In kind consideration. My arrangements demand it."

"Do let the girl go," said Van Diemen. "Dine with me tonight and I'll give you a wine to brisk your spirits, old boy"

"Thank you. When I have ordered dinner at home, I——and my wine agrees with ME," Tinman replied.

"I doubt it."

"You shall not provoke me, Philip."

They parted stiffly.

Mrs. Cavely had unpleasant domestic news to communicate to her brother, in return for his tale of affliction and wrath. It concerned the ungrateful conduct of their little housemaid Jane, who, as Mrs. Cavely said, "egged on by that woman Crickledon," had been hinting at an advance of wages.

"She didn't dare speak, but I saw what was in her when she broke a plate, and wouldn't say she was sorry. I know she goes to Crickledon and talks us over. She's a willing worker, but she has no heart."

Tinman had been accustomed in his shop at Helmstone—where heaven had blessed him with the patronage of the rich, as visibly as rays of supernal light are seen selecting from above the heads of prophets in the illustrations to cheap holy books—to deal with willing workers that have no hearts. Before the application for an advance of wages—and he knew the signs of it coming—his method was to calculate how much he might be asked for, and divide the estimated sum; which, as it seemed to come from a generous impulse, and had been unsolicited, was often humbly accepted, and the willing worker pursued her lean and hungry course in his service. The treatment did not always agree with his males. Women it suited; because they do not like to lift up their voices unless they are in a passion; and if you take from them the grounds of temper, you take their words away — you make chickens of them. And as Tinman said, "Gratitude I never expect!" Why not? For the reason that he knew human nature. He could record shocking instances of the ingratitude of human nature, as revealed to him in the term of his tenure of the shop at Helmstone. Blest from above, human nature's wickedness had from below too frequently besulphured and suffumigated him for his memory to be dim; and though he was ever ready to own himself an example that heaven prevaileth, he could cite instances of scandalmongering shop-women dismissed and working him mischief in the town, which pointed to him in person for a proof that the Powers of Good and Evil were still engaged in unhappy contention. Witness Strikes! witness Revolutions!

"Tell her, when she lays the cloth, that I advance her, on account of general good conduct, five shillings per annum. Add," said Tinman, "that I wish no thanks. It is for her merits — to reward her; you understand me, Martha?"

"Quite; if you think it prudent, Martin."

"I do. She is not to breathe a syllable to cook."

"She will."

"Then keep your eye on cook."

Mrs. Cavely promised she would do so. She felt sure she was paying five shillings for ingratitude; and, therefore, it was with humility that she owned her error when, while her brother sipped his sugared acrid liquor after dinner (in devotion to the doctor's decree, that he should take a couple of glasses, rigorously as body-lashing friar), she imparted to him the singular effect of the advance of wages upon little Jane — "Oh, ma'am! and me never asked you for it!" She informed her brother how little Jane had confided to her that they were called "close," and how little Jane had vowed she would — the willing little thing! — go about letting everybody know their kindness.

"Yes! Ah!" Tinman inhaled the praise. "No, no; I don't want to be puffed," he said. "Remember cook. I have," he continued, meditatively, "rarely found my plan fail. But mind, I give the Crickledons notice to quit to-morrow. They are a pest. Besides, I shall probably think of erecting villas."

"How dreadful the wind is!" Mrs. Cavely exclaimed. "I would give that girl Annette one chance more. Try her by letter."

Tinman despatched a business letter to Annette, which brought back a vague, unbusiness-like reply. Two days afterward Mrs. Cavely reported to her brother the presence of Mr. Fellingham and Miss Mary Fellingham in Crikswich. At her dictation he wrote a second letter. This time the reply came from Van Diemen:

"My DEAR MARTIN, — Please do not go on bothering my girl. She does
not like the idea of leaving me, and my experience tells me I could
not live in the house with you. So there it is. Take it friendly.
I have always wanted to be, and am,
"Your friend,
"PHIL."

Tinman proceeded straight to Elba; that is, as nearly straight as the wind would allow his legs to walk. Van Diemen was announced to be out; Miss Annette begged to be excused, under the pretext that she was unwell; and Tinman heard of a dinner-party at Elba that night.

He met Mr. Fellingham on the carriage drive. The young Londoner presumed to touch upon Tinman's private affairs by pleading on behalf of the Crikledons, who were, he said, much dejected by the notice they had received to quit house and shop.

"Another time," bawled Tinman. "I can't hear you in this wind."

"Come in," said Fellingham.

"The master of the house is absent," was the smart retort roared at him; and Tinman staggered away, enjoying it as he did his wine.

His house rocked. He was backed by his sister in the assurance that he had been duped.

The process he supposed to be thinking, which was the castigation of his brains with every sting wherewith a native touchiness could ply immediate recollection, led him to conclude that he must bring Van Diemen to his senses, and Annette running to him for mercy.

He sat down that night amid the howling of the storm, wind whistling, water crashing, casements rattling, beach desperately dragging, as by the wide-stretched star-fish fingers of the half-engulphed.

He hardly knew what he wrote. The man was in a state of personal terror, burning with indignation at Van Diemen as the main cause of his jeopardy. For, in order to prosecute his pursuit of Annette, he had abstained from going to Helmstone to pay moneys into his bank there, and what was precious to life as well as life itself, was imperilled by those two— Annette and her father—who, had they been true, had they been honest, to say nothing of honourable, would by this time have opened Elba to him as a fast and safe abode.

His letter was addressed, on a large envelope,

"To the Adjutant-General,

"HORSE GUARDS."

But if ever consigned to the Post, that post-office must be in London; and Tinman left the letter on his desk till the morning should bring counsel to him as to the London friend to whom he might despatch it under cover for posting, if he pushed it so far.

Sleep was impossible. Black night favoured the tearing fiends of shipwreck, and looking through a back window over sea, Tinman saw with dismay huge towering ghostwhite wreaths, that travelled up swiftly on his level, and lit the dark as they flung themselves in ruin, with a gasp, across the mound of shingle at his feet.

He undressed: His sister called to him to know if they were in danger. Clothed in his dressing-gown, he slipped along to her door, to vociferate to her hoarsely that she must not frighten the servants; and one fine quality in the training of the couple, which had helped them to prosper, a form of self-command, kept her quiet in her shivering fears.

For a distraction Tinman pulled open the drawers of his wardrobe. His glittering suit lay in one. And he thought, "What wonderful changes there are in the world!" meaning, between a man exposed to the wrath of the elements, and the same individual reading from vellum, in that suit, in a palace, to the Head of all of us!

The presumption is; that he must have often done it before. The fact is established, that he did it that night. The conclusion drawn from it is, that it must have given him a sense of stability and safety.

At any rate that he put on the suit is quite certain.

Probably it was a work of ingratiation and degrees; a feeling of the silk, a trying on to one leg, then a matching of the fellow with it. O you Revolutionists! who would have no state, no ceremonial, and but one order of galligaskins! This man must have been wooed away in spirit to forgetfulness of the tempest scourging his mighty neighbour to a bigger and a farther leap; he must have obtained from the contemplation of himself in his suit that which would be the saving of all men, in especial of his countrymen—imagination, namely.

Certain it is, as I have said, that he attired himself in the suit. He covered it with his dressing-gown, and he lay down on his bed so garbed, to await the morrow's light, being probably surprised by sleep acting upon fatigue and nerves appeased and soothed.

CHAPTER XII

Elba lay more sheltered from South-east winds under the slopes of down than any other house in Crikswich. The South-caster struck off the cliff to a martello tower and the house on the beach, leaving Elba to repose, so that the worst wind for that coast was one of the most comfortable for the owner of the hall, and he looked from his upper window on a sea of crumbling grey chalk, lashed unremittingly by the featureless piping gale, without fear that his elevated grounds and walls would be open at high tide to the ravage of water. Van Diemen had no idea of calamity being at work on land when he sat down to breakfast. He told Herbert that he had prayed for poor fellows at sea last night. Mary Fellingham and Annette were anxious to finish breakfast and mount the down to gaze on the sea, and receiving a caution from Van Diemen not to go too near the cliff, they were inclined to think he was needlessly timorous on their account.

Before they were half way through the meal, word was brought in of great breaches in the shingle, and water covering the common. Van Diemen sent for his head gardener, whose report of the state of things outside took the comprehensive form of prophecy; he predicted the fall of the town.

"Nonsense; what do you mean, John Scott?" said Van Diemen, eyeing his orderly breakfast table and the man in turns. "It does n't seem like that, yet, does it?"

"The house on the beach won't stand an hour longer, sir."

"Who says so?"

"It's cut off from land now, and waves mast-high all about it."

"Mart Tinman?" cried Van Diemen.

All started; all jumped up; and there was a scampering for hats and cloaks. Maids and men of the house ran in and out confirming the news of inundation. Some in terror for the fate of relatives, others pleasantly excited, glad of catastrophe if it but killed monotony, for at any rate it was a change of demons.

The view from the outer bank of Elba was of water covering the space of the common up to the stones of Marine Parade and Belle Vue. But at a distance it had not the appearance of angry water; the ladies thought it picturesque, and the house on the beach was seen standing firm. A second look showed the house completely isolated; and as the party led by Van Diemen circled hurriedly toward the town, they discerned heavy cataracts of foam pouring down the wrecked mound of shingle on either side of the house.

"Why, the outer wall's washed away," said Van Diemen." Are they in real danger?" asked Annette, her teeth chattering, and the cold and other matters at her heart precluding for the moment such warmth of sympathy as she hoped soon to feel for them. She was glad to hear her father say:

"Oh! they're high and dry by this time. We shall find them in the town And we'll take them in and comfort them. Ten to one they have n't breakfasted. They sha'n't go to an inn while I'm handy."

He dashed ahead, followed closely by Herbert. The ladies beheld them talking to townsfolk as they passed along the upper streets, and did not augur well of their increase of speed. At the head of the town water was visible, part of the way up the main street, and crossing it, the ladies went swiftly under the old church, on the tower of which were spectators, through the churchyard to a high meadow that dropped to a stone wall fixed between the meadow and a grass bank above the level of the road, where now salt water beat and cast some spray. Not less than a hundred people were in this field, among them Crickledon and his wife. All were in silent watch of the house on the beach, which was to east of the field, at a distance of perhaps three stonethrows. The scene was wild. Continuously the torrents poured through the shingleclefts, and momently a thunder sounded, and high leapt a billow that topped the house and folded it weltering.

"They tell me Mart Tinman's in the house," Van Diemen roared to Herbert.
He listened to further information, and bellowed: "There's no boat!"

Herbert answered: "It must be a mistake, I think; here's Crickledon says he had a warning before dawn and managed to move most of his things, and the people over there must have been awakened by the row in time to get off"

"I can't hear a word you say;" Van Diemen tried to pitch his voice higher than the wind. "Did you say a boat? But where?"

Crickledon the carpenter made signal to Herbert. They stepped rapidly up the field.

"Women feels their weakness in times like these, my dear," Mrs. Crickledon said to Annette. "What with our clothes and our cowardice it do seem we're not the equals of men when winds is high."

Annette expressed the hope to her that she had not lost much property. Mrs. Crickledon said she was glad to let her know she was insured in an Accident Company. "But," said she, "I do grieve for that poor man Tinman, if alive he be, and comes ashore to find his property wrecked by water. Bless ye! he wouldn't insure against anything less common than fire; and my house and Crickledon's shop are floating timbers by this time; and Marine Parade and Belle Vue are safe to go. And it'll be a pretty welcome for him, poor man, from his investments."

A cry at a tremendous blow of a wave on the doomed house rose from the field. Back and front door were broken down, and the force of water drove a round volume through the channel, shaking the walls.

"I can't stand this," Van Diemen cried.

Annette was too late to hold him back. He ran up the field. She was preparing to run after when Mrs. Crickledon touched her arm and implored her: "Interfere not with men, but let them follow their judgements when it's seasons of mighty peril, my dear. If any one's guilty it's me, for minding my husband of a boat that was launched for a life-boat here, and wouldn't answer, and is at the shed by the Crouch—left lying there, I've often said, as if it was a-sulking. My goodness!"

A linen sheet bad been flung out from one of the windows of the house on the beach, and flew loose and flapping in sign of distress.

"It looks as if they had gone mad in that house, to have waited so long for to declare theirselves, poor souls," Mrs. Crickledon said, sighing.

She was assured right and left that signals had been seen before, and some one stated that the cook of Mr. Tinman, and also Mrs. Cavely, were on shore.

"It's his furniture, poor man, he sticks to: and nothing gets round the heart so!" resumed Mrs. Crickledon. "There goes his bed-linen!"

The sheet was whirled and snapped away by the wind; distended doubled, like a flock of winter geese changeing alphabetical letters on the clouds, darted this way and that, and finally outspread on the waters breaking against Marine Parade.

"They cannot have thought there was positive danger in remaining," said
Annette.

"Mr. Tinman was waiting for the cheapest Insurance office," a man remarked to Mrs. Crickledon.

"The least to pay is to the undertaker," she replied, standing on tiptoe. "And it's to be hoped he 'll pay more to-day. If only those walls don't fall and stop the chance of the boat to save him for more outlay, poor man! What boats was on the beach last night, high up and over the ridge as they was, are planks by this time and only good for carpenters."

"Half our town's done for," one old man said; and another followed him in. a pious tone: "From water we came and to water we go."

They talked of ancient inroads of the sea, none so serious as this threatened to be for them. The gallant solidity, of the house on the beach had withstood heavy gales: it was a brave house. Heaven be thanked, no fishing boats were out. Chiefly well-to-do people would be the sufferers—an exceptional case. For it is the mysterious and unexplained dispensation that: "Mostly heaven chastises we."

A knot of excited gazers drew the rest of the field to them. Mrs. Crickledon, on the edge of the crowd, reported what was doing to Annette and Miss Fellingham. A boat had been launched from the town. "Praise the Lord, there's none but coastguard in it!" she exclaimed, and excused herself for having her heart on her husband.

Annette was as deeply thankful that her father was not in the boat.

They looked round and saw Herbert beside them. Van Diemen was in the rear, panting, and straining his neck to catch sight of the boat now pulling fast across a tumbled sea to where Tinman himself was perceived, beckoning them wildly, half out of one of the windows.

"A pound apiece to those fellows, and two if they land Mart Tinman dry; I've promised it, and they'll earn it. Look at that! Quick, you rascals!"

To the east a portion of the house had fallen, melted away. Where it stood, just below the line of shingle, it was now like a structure wasting on a tormented submerged reef. The whole line was given over to the waves.

"Where is his sister?" Annette shrieked to her father.

"Safe ashore; and one of the women with her. But Mart Tinman would stop, the fool! to-poor old boy! save his papers and things; and has n't a head to do it, Martha Cavely tells me. They're at him now! They've got him in! There's another? Oh! it's a girl, who would n't go and leave him. They'll pull to the field here. Brave lads! — By jingo, why ain't Englishmen always in danger! — eh? if you want to see them shine!"

"It's little Jane," said Mrs. Crickledon, who had been joined by her husband, and now that she knew him to be no longer in peril, kept her hand on him to restrain him, just for comfort's sake.

The boat held under the lee of the house-wreck a minute; then, as if shooting a small rapid, came down on a wave crowned with foam, to hurrahs from the townsmen.

"They're all right," said Van Diemen, puffing as at a mist before his eyes. "They'll pull westward, with the wind, and land him among us. I remember when old Mart and I were bathing once, he was younger than me, and could n't swim much, and I saw him going down. It'd have been hard to see him washed off before one's eyes thirty years afterwards. Here they come. He's all right. He's in his dressing-gown!"

The crowd made way for Mr. Van Diemen Smith to welcome his friend. Two of the coastguard jumped out, and handed him to the dry bank, while Herbert, Van Diemen, and Crickledon took him by hand and arm, and hoisted him on to the flint wall, preparatory to his descent into the field. In this exposed situation the wind, whose pranks are endless when it is once up, seized and blew Martin Tinman's dressing-gown wide as two violently flapping wings on each side of him, and finally over his head.

Van Diemen turned a pair of stupefied flat eyes on Herbert, who cast a sly look at the ladies. Tinman had sprung down. But not before the. world, in one tempestuous glimpse, had caught sight of the Court suit.

Perfect gravity greeted him from the crowd.

"Safe, old Mart! and glad to be able to say it," said Van Diemen.

"We are so happy," said Annette.

"House, furniture, property, everything I possess!" ejaculated Tinman, shivering.

"Fiddle, man; you want some hot breakfast in you. Your sister has gone on — to Elba. Come you too, old Man; and where's that plucky little girl who stood by — "

"Was there a girl?" said Tinman.

"Yes, and there was a boy wanted to help." Van Diemen pointed at Herbert.

Tinman looked, and piteously asked, "Have you examined Marine Parade and
Belle Vue? It depends on the tide!"

"Here is little Jane, sir," said Mrs. Crickledon.

"Fall in," Van Diemen said to little Jane.

The girl was bobbing curtseys to Annette, on her introduction by Mrs. Crickledon.

"Martin, you stay at my house; you stay at Elba till you get things comfortable about you, and then you shall have the Crouch for a year, rent free. Eh, Netty?"

Annette chimed in: "Anything we can do, anything. Nothing can be too much."

Van Diemen was praising little Jane for her devotion to her master.

"Master have been so kind to me," said little Jane.

"Now, march; it is cold," Van Diemen gave the word, and Herbert stood by Mary rather dejectedly, foreseeing that his prospects at Elba were darkened.

"Now then, Mart, left leg forward," Van Diemen linked his arm in his friend's.

"I must have a look," Tinman broke from him, and cast a forlorn look of farewell on the last of the house on the beach.

"You've got me left to you, old Mart; don't forget that," said Van Diemen.

Tinman's chest fell. "Yes, yes," he responded. He was touched.

"And I told those fellows if they landed you dry they should have—I'd give them double pay; and I do believe they've earned their money."

"I don't think I'm very wet, I'm cold," said Tinman.

"You can't help being cold, so come along."

"But, Philip!" Tinman lifted his voice; "I've lost everything. I tried to save a little. I worked hard, I exposed my life, and all in vain."

The voice of little Jane was heard.

"What's the matter with the child?" said Van Diemen.

Annette went up to her quietly.

But little Jane was addressing her master.

"Oh! if you please, I did manage to save something the last thing when the boat was at the window, and if you please, sir, all the bundles is lost, but I saved you a papercutter, and a letter Horse Guards, and here they are, sir."

The grateful little creature drew the square letter and paper-cutter from her bosom, and held them out to Mr. Tinman.

It was a letter of the imposing size, with THE HORSE GUARDS very distinctly inscribed on it in Tinman's best round hand, to strike his vindictive spirit as positively intended for transmission, and give him sight of his power to wound if it pleased him; as it might.

"What!" cried he, not clearly comprehending how much her devotion had accomplished for him.

"A letter to the Horse Guards!" cried Van Diemen.

"Here, give it me," said little Jane's master, and grasped it nervously.

"What's in that letter?" Van Diemen asked. "Let me look at that letter. Don't tell me it's private correspondence."

"My dear Philip, dear friend, kind thanks; it's not a letter," said Tinman.

"Not a letter! why, I read the address, 'Horse Guards.' I read it as it passed into your hands. Now, my man, one look at that letter, or take the consequences."

"Kind thanks for your assistance, dear Philip, indeed! Oh! this? Oh! it's nothing." He tore it in halves.

His face was of the winter sea-colour, with the chalk wash on it.

"Tear again, and I shall know what to think of the contents," Van Diemen frowned. "Let me see what you've said. You've sworn you would do it, and there it is at last, by miracle; but let me see it and I'll overlook it, and you shall be my house-mate still. If not! — —"

Tinman tore away.

"You mistake, you mistake, you're entirely wrong," he said, as he pursued with desperation his task of rendering every word unreadable.

Van Diemen stood fronting him; the accumulation of stores of petty injuries and meannesses which he had endured from this man, swelled under the whip of the conclusive exhibition of treachery. He looked so black that Annette called, "Papa!"

"Philip," said Tinman. "Philip! my best friend!"

"Pooh, you're a poor creature. Come along and breakfast at Elba, and you can sleep at the Crouch, and goodnight to you. Crickledon," he called to the houseless couple, "you stop at Elba till I build you a shop."

With these words, Van Diemen led the way, walking alone. Herbert was compelled to walk with Tinman.

Mary and Annette came behind, and Mary pinched Annette's arm so sharply that she must have cried out aloud had it been possible for her to feel pain at that moment, instead of a personal exultation, flying wildly over the clash of astonishment and horror, like a sea-bird over the foam.

In the first silent place they came to, Mary murmured the words: "Little Jane."

Annette looked round at Mrs. Crickledon, who wound up the procession, taking little Jane by the hand. Little Jane was walking demurely, with a placid face. Annette glanced at Tinman. Her excited feelings nearly rose to a scream of laughter. For hours after, Mary had only to say to her: "Little Jane," to produce the same convulsion. It rolled her heart and senses in a headlong surge, shook her to burning tears, and seemed to her ideas the most wonderful running together of opposite things ever known on this earth. The young lady was ashamed of her laughter; but she was deeply indebted to it, for never was mind made so clear by that beneficent exercise.